UMBERTO SABA

# ERNESTO

*translated from the Italian*
*by Mark Thompson*

CARCANET

First published in Great Britain 1987 by
Carcanet Press Limited
208–212 Corn Exchange Buildings
Manchester M4 3BQ

Carcanet
198 Sixth Avenue
New York, New York 10013

**British Library Cataloguing in Publication Data**

Saba, Umberto
   Ernesto.
   I. Title
   853'.912 [F]        PQ4841.A18

   ISBN 0-85635-559-3


The publisher acknowledges the financial assistance
of the Arts Council of Great Britain

Typeset in 12/13½pt Bembo by Paragon Photoset, Aylesbury
Printed in England by SRP Ltd, Exeter

# CONTENTS

# Preface

If the Adriatic city of Trieste has literary associations for you, English-speaking reader, it is as good as certain that they involve James Joyce; and that if they stretch to a second name, it will be Italo Svevo. Yet beyond its fame as the rock of Promethejoyce ('And trieste, ah trieste ate I my liver' — but he also called it 'my second country'), and the habitat of Zeno, Trieste was the birthplace, home, muse and perennial theme of Umberto Saba, the last of the great Italian poets of this century to reach a foreign audience. Or rather, an English-speaking one: elsewhere he has been read and admired for decades, by Camus, Neruda and Gide among others. Cultural chauvinism apart, this is not accidental: Saba's spare lyric poetry is hardly translatable out of Latin languages, though Felix Stefanile has produced some beautiful English versions, several of which I quote in my Notes with gratitude and pleasure.

Saba is as familiar to Italians as Yeats and Robert Frost are to us; every school child reads some poems from his *Canzoniere* (literally, 'song book'), in which his many separate volumes are collected. Each of Saba's several hundred poems needs to be read and felt as one fragment of this book, which is, in a special sense, a life's work: that is, a body of writing which *declares* itself to be inseparable from the life and experiences of the author. For Saba, what other poets would treat as the raw material of poetry is the very subject of poetry. He was suspicious of the stylistic conventions and trademarks which are so important to modernist art; hermeticism and symbolism, for example, he disparaged as devices for evasion, and if good work was done under their banners, it was despite not because of the doctrine.

In 1953, in a seventieth-birthday tribute, Pasolini wrote about the shape of the *Canzionere*, the way it reflects and recreates the contours of a human life: 'Saba is a poet in perpetual self-making (*in continuo farsi*) . . . Always and forever risking failure and relapse, he has to begin each time, painfully, at the beginning, always experimenting. But this is why, now, on his seventieth birthday, we can say that he has truly exhausted his subject—has raised the life of his emotions into poetry.'

*Ernesto* was Saba's secret book. Begun a few weeks after that seventieth birthday and read aloud to a few friends, but always considered unpublishable by its author, *Ernesto* was a *succès de scandale et d'estime* when it was brought out by Einaudi in 1975 (often reprinted, it has predictably been 'adapted' into a film). By 1953 Saba had almost stopped writing poetry, so Pasolini could not know that his subject was not quite exhausted; that he would yet write this loving celebration of freedom, poetry, and 'the marvellous world'.

The Afterword presents Saba's comments on *Ernesto*, culled from his letters, and then takes issue with their view of the story.

There are several reasons why the Notes are so numerous and long-winded. Saba's writing being what it is, *Ernesto* will mean more to the reader if s/he has even a sketchy idea of its place in his work. Also, it was never meant for publication; the private jokes and loose ends are less irritating, more appealing, if they are annotated. Lastly, there is no reason why readers should know anything much of the history and culture of Trieste, in which this story is deeply embedded (and which, incidentally, are increasingly fashionable academic topics in Italy). *Ernesto* is simply more rewarding if some of this rich background can be given.

The aim in the Notes is to cite as wide a range of opinions on these little-known matters as I practically can; hence all the quotation. They are enthusiastic rather than scholarly, meant to amplify not analyse, and work best — I think — if they are read straight through after the story.

Mark Thompson
November 1986

# First Episode

Now that I am old, I should like simply to describe,
with serene innocence, the marvellous world.

from 'The Immaculate Gentleman in White'
in *Ricordi-Racconti*

What's up? Are you tired?
   Fed up.
   Who with?
   The boss. What a shark — just one and a half florins
for loading and unloading two carts.
   Terrible, you're right.
   This conversation (which I set down in dialect, like
the ones which follow, though the dialect is toned
down as much as possible in the hope that the reader —
if this story ever has a reader — can translate it for
himself) took place in Trieste at the very end of the
nineteenth century between a man and a boy. The man
— a day-labourer — was sitting on a pile of flour sacks
in a warehouse on the Via ——. He wore a red kerchief
round his head and down to his shoulders to protect his
neck from the coarse sacking. He was still young,
though it was true he looked tired, and there was
something of the gypsy in his features, but thoroughly
softened and domesticated. Ernesto was sixteen years
old, an apprentice in this business which bought flour
from the big Hungarian mills and sold it to the bakers
in the city. He had hazel eyes (just the colour of some
poodles' eyes) and light, curly chestnut hair, and he
walked with a loose-limbed adolescent grace — the
kind that always thinks itself graceless and fears itself

ridiculous. Just now he was standing up, leaning against the open door of the warehouse, waiting for the cart to return with the last load of the day — it was due any moment — and looking at the man as if he had never seen him before; yet he had known and been talking to him for months, because they worked together and also because he rather liked him. The man propped his head on his hands, as a man does when he is tired or angry.

You're right, Ernesto said again, the boss is a real skinflint and I hate him too (but looking more closely, no one would think this boy could hate anybody), and when he sends me to the Piazza to hire a man and tells me he'll pay so much and no more, my heart sinks. I always fetch you, but I'm ashamed I have to offer you so little. That's the job I like least, I can tell you.

The man stirred from his gloomy position and looked warmly at Ernesto. You're a good lad, I know, he said, and if you ever become a boss, as I hope you will, I'm sure you won't treat your workers like your boss treats me. The man's a crook — one and a half florins for three cartloads, and only two of us for the job — it's daylight robbery, no question. He doesn't know what it means to wear yourself out, and it's worse now with summer on the way. Even two florins each wouldn't be enough, and if it wasn't that I like talking to you I wouldn't be waiting for this cart: I'd knock off now — go straight home to bed.

It was a day towards the end of spring and the street outside was bright with sun. But it was cool inside the warehouse, cool, damp and smelling of flour.

Why don't you come and sit down? the man suggested after a pause, gesturing to a place beside his own. There's a room here; you can sit on my jacket if you're worried about the dirt. And he made as if to spread out his jacket, for he was already in shirtsleeves, waiting for the cart.

No need for that, Ernesto replied. Flour isn't dirty, you can brush it off so it doesn't leave any marks. And even if it did I wouldn't care what people saw. He stopped the man unfolding his jacket and sat down beside him, smiling. The man smiled back; he did not look tired or angry any longer.

I'll dust you off after, he said, if you'll let me.

They looked at one another for a while in silence.

You're a good lad, said the man for the second time. Handsome too, so handsome it's a pleasure just to look at you.

Me handsome? Ernesto laughed. No one ever said that before.

Not your mother even?

Her least of all. I can't remember the last time she gave me a kiss or hugged me. She still says what she's always said: you mustn't spoil sons.

Would you've liked her to kiss you?

When I was a kid, yes. I don't care now, but I'd have been glad if she'd said something nice once in a while.

Didn't that happen either?

Never, Ernesto replied. Or hardly ever.

A pity I'm so poor and don't have any decent clothes.

Why?

Because otherwise I'd like us to be friends. We could have gone for a walk one weekend.

I'm not rich either — d'you know how much I earn?

No, but you've got parents and they must have money. So how much do you earn?

Thirty crowns a month, and twenty of those go to my mother. She buys my clothes, it's true (Ernesto's clothes were always bought off-the-peg; while he would have been loath to admit it, he might have liked to dress smartly, as some of his old schoolmates had done), so there isn't much left for me.

But you're learning as well in the meantime.

I don't like having a job at all. I'd like to be doing something completely different.

Like what?

This time the boy made no reply.

So how do you spend your ten crowns? Do they go on women? (The second question was asked as if fearing an affirmative answer.)

No, I don't go with women yet — I've decided not to have anything to do with them till I'm eighteen or nineteen. (Perhaps he had forgotten that two years before, his mother had had to give notice to a young servant girl whom Ernesto was forever pestering in the kitchen. After that the poor woman made sure to employ only misshapen, ugly old women: she collected a real gallery of hags. But they never stayed long, always leaving or being dismissed after a month or two.)

What about you? he asked. Are you married?

The man laughed. Not me, I'm single — don't bother with girls.

How old are you?

Twenty-eight . . . I look more, don't you think?

Not at all, no. I'm sixteen, nearly seventeen — seventeen next month.

Don't you want to tell me what you do with your ten crowns a month?

Aren't you nosy, Ernest laughed. They soon go, either in cake shops or on theatre tickets. I go to the theatre most Sundays after supper. I like tragedies best. Don't you ever go to the theatre?

What would I be doing, going to the theatre? I was brought up an orphan, I don't have a clue about things like that — I can hardly read or write my own name.

I love the theatre, Ernesto went on, like every other

boy in the world (and not only the boys), too concerned with himself to think about other people. Last Sunday I saw *The Robbers* by Schiller, it was wonderful.

Was it funny? asked the man absently.

No! I cried. I was in a bad way, I went home in such a state my mother said she'd never let me go to the theatre again: it's wasting money if I only come home all upset.

Don't you have a father?

How did you know?

You only ever mention your mother, the man said almost apologetically.

I never knew my father.

Is he dead? asked the man in a low voice.

No, separated from my mother. They separated six months before I was born.

Why?

Don't know. They quarrelled. So I've never seen my father. He lives in another city, and I don't think he's even allowed back to Trieste. Not that I mind not seeing him: he can stay where he is for all I care.

So you live alone with your mother.

With her and my old aunt. The aunt's the one with the money, and she's careful to keep it that way. There's my uncle too — he's my guardian as well, but he doesn't live with us, he's married. He only comes for Sunday lunch, which is all too often for me. He's crazy.

Crazy?

Round the bend. A few days ago he wanted to clout me round the head — as if I was still ten years old! (Ernesto stroked his cheek with the back of his hand as he spoke; obviously the threat had been made good, and the boy was ashamed to admit it.)

What had you done?

Nothing. We had an argument after lunch about politics, and I'm always for the socialists. What about you?

I told you I don't know about things like that, and anyway I don't care about politics. But it's good that you're for the socialists.

Why d'you think so?

Because lads like you always take the bosses' side.

Not me, I can't stand men who exploit other men's labour.

Is that what you told your uncle?

That and more. He's mad but he's not really nasty; he gave me a florin after he clouted me. He's been giving me florins every week for three years, and last Sunday he gave me an extra one. Perhaps he was sorry; but as I say, he's more mad than bad.

Well then, mightn't it be better if he clouts you every week? asked the man with a laugh.

No, I don't like being hit. Not for my sake, because of my mother. It hurts her every time, and she's very fond of her brother.

She's very fond of you too — more than you think. How could she live with you and not be?

Why are you saying these things?

The man put his hand on the boy's hand, which lay palm down on the sacking. He seemed tense.

What a pity! he said, and looked surprised and glad when the boy did not take his hand away.

What's a pity?

What I said before, about us being friends and going for walks together.

Because you're much older than me?

No.

Because you haven't got smart clothes? I told you before, things like that don't matter. So . . .

The man fell silent. He seemed to be struggling with

himself, as if he wanted to say something and wanted not to say it. Ernesto felt the man's hand trembling on top of his own. Then — as someone risking his all to win everything — he looked the boy straight in the eye and burst out in a strange voice:

But do you know what it means for a boy like you to be friends with a man like me? Because if you don't, I'm not the one who's going to tell you.

He was briefly silent again. Then, when the boy blushed and looked at the floor but still did not move his hand, he added almost aggressively:

*Do* you know?

Ernesto slid his hand from the man's grasp, which had tightened and become damp with sweat, and laid it timidly on the man's leg. He drew his hand up and along till, lightly and as if by chance, it brushed his sex. Then he looked boldly up at the man, a luminous smile on his face.

The man felt overwhelmed. His mouth was dry and his heart was pounding so hard he felt faint, and all he could say was:

Do you see? — which seemed addressed more to himself than to the boy.

There was a long silence, which Ernesto broke by answering:

I do see, yes, but . . . where?

What do you mean, where? the man asked vaguely. It was Ernesto who seemed the more prompt of the two.

If we're going to do things we shouldn't do, don't we have to be alone?

Of course.

So where do you want us to go to be alone? asked Ernesto in a low voice, some of his bravado already draining away.

Tonight, out in the country, I know a place . . .

I can't in the evening.

Why not? Do you go to bed early?

If only I could! I'm half-asleep on my feet by then. No, I have to go to night school.

Can't you skip it once?

No, my mother comes too.

Is she worried you wouldn't go?

I don't think so, she knows I don't lie to her. It's an excuse for her to get some exercise. She wants me to learn shorthand and German: she always says you can't get ahead without German . . . Anyway I'd be scared to go out in the country.

Scared of me?

No, not of you.

Of what then? If it's these clothes you're ashamed of, I can wear my Sunday best.

Someone might come past and see us.

Not in the place I'm thinking of.

I'd still be scared . . . Why not here in the warehouse?

But there are always people around, they'd get suspicious if we started coming out of here together (Ernesto had keys to the building and the man knew it). The boss lives right across the street, worse luck. And his wife's never away from the window, and she's even worse than him.

Can't we find an excuse? Like pretending you've left something behind? Whenever there's a job that needs finishing urgently I come back to the office after lunch at two o'clock instead of three, before it's time to open. That's partly why the boss gives me the keys. Sometimes I'm here by myself more than an hour, and you could always say . . . Oh look, here's the cart!

They saw first the heads, then the flanks of two powerful dray-horses framed in the open doorway. Then the cart with the carter on foot, holding the whip and reins. Before the horses could obey the carter's *Whoa!* a second man, fat and heavily built, jumped down from the sacks where he was sitting cross-legged like a Turk, and hailed the man in a slurred voice. He had come to help unload.

Let's talk later, said the man, hurried and hoarse. He had taken off the red kerchief during their conversation; now he knotted it again behind his head and set to work. His legs trembled beneath him slightly as he went.


After the two men had unloaded all the sacks (not without oaths and abuse from the fat one), with Ernesto entering and marking them one by one, a furious argument flared up in the office. Cesco, the fat man, started it; for all his damning and blasting he must have been drinking even more than usual. Ernesto's friend, on the other hand, was in no mood to argue about anything; he wanted only one thing now: to get to the fried-food shop as quickly as possible, eat whatever was on the slate that day, then go straight home to lie down and think. For months (since setting eyes on Ernesto, in fact) he had been hoping for what had just happened (rather, for what promised to happen soon) and he was (if anyone can ever call himself . . .) happy. But his happiness was not unqualified: might not the boy have second thoughts, or take offence afterwards, or foolishly spill the whole story to a third party? So he would have taken whatever the boss had offered through Ernesto when he came to find him in the Piazza — would have accepted it without batting an eyelid. It even seemed to him that his paltry wages had grown much bigger, for Ernesto had told him the rate, not fixed it himself. But the fat man did not have his reasons to keep quiet, and anyway he was drunk. The boss was defending himself in his horrible Italian, which always betrayed his origins: he was an Hungarian Jew with a passion for Germany, where, so he said, he had been educated, then lived for some years. Ernesto was especially irritated by his accent — it was torture to his ears, for he was proud of being a good Italian as well as a good socialist. He had read the lives of Garibaldi and Victor Emmanuel II when he was a little boy: in those days the only books in the house, forgotten by his guardian uncle since his own youth. The word *Germany* was positively insulting to Ernesto, and it was a word his employer used often (as often as possible), mispronouncing it *Chermany* and praising the peerless virtues of its people. Still, the man had to show solidarity and support his mate, and Cesco's threats eventually prevailed over Signor Wilder's meanness, which, while not actually breaking the law (there weren't any laws to protect any workers at that time, let alone day-labourers), did go against the accepted practice in the Piazza. With a bad grace he raised the wage: now and in future the two men would have four florins between them instead of three. (Two florins each — exactly the amount Ernesto's friend had mentioned before.) The man was already on his way out when the boss called him back to say there would be work the next day. He engaged him for the whole afternoon and said to come an hour before opening time, as it would not be possible to take the goods to their destination before three o'clock and there were a good many leaking sacks that needed mending. He would (he said through gritted teeth) pay for the extra time. Signor Wilder was very suspicious by nature and never left a worker on the premises without Ernesto there to supervise, so he told the boy he must be in the office by two o'clock as well. It was fate, speaking — it so happened — through

Signor Wilder's lips, and in a manner as sudden as it was irresistible. They both knew it immediately; neither dared look at the other. Yet the man's eyes were shining, and he swallowed softly. He left straightaway, barely saying goodbye, and the boy busied himself with the letter-book. But his thoughts too were elsewhere . . .

Now we're alone, said the man, when he realized that Ernesto was not going to speak. Out of the bag he always brought to work he had taken a needle and thread to sew the sacks, but he was really waiting for the boy to say something to recall their conversation of the day before — something to encourage him. But Ernesto did not so much as open his mouth. He had positioned himself nearby (nearer than usual, perhaps) and stood staring at the floor, fiddling with the paper label on one of the sacks until it came off in his hand. He tore the label into shreds and tossed the shreds away.

Alone, he said at last. Alone for an hour.

There are lots of things you can do in an hour, the man added readily.

What things do you mean?

Don't you remember what we talked about yesterday? What you as good as promised me? Don't you know what I'm so longing to do with you?

You want to put it up my arse, Ernesto said with serene innocence.

The man was taken aback to hear this crude phrase from a boy like Ernesto. He was hurt as well — hurt and frightened. He thought the kid, already regretting his half-consent, was mocking him. Worse yet, he might have told somebody or — worst of all — confessed to his mother. But the truth was quite different.

Without being aware of it himself, the boy's clear answer showed what many years later, after much experience and much suffering, would become his own 'style': his reaching to the heart of things, to the red-hot core of life, overcoming dogma and inhibition without evasion or word-spinning, whether he was treating low, coarse subjects (even forbidden ones) or those which people call sublime, putting them all on the same level, as Nature does. But none of this was on his mind at the time: his mouth spoke the words (which almost made the labourer blush) because the situation called for them. He wanted to please his friend and make him happy, and he wanted to experience those new sensations — wanted them *for* their novelty and strangeness. At the same time he was afraid it might hurt. And this, just then, was all that frightened him.

Is it *so* good? he asked.

The best thing in the world.

Maybe for you, but I . . .

For you too . . . Haven't you ever done it with a man before?

Me? Never . . . Have you with other boys?

Often, but none were as handsome as you. He reached out to touch the boy, who drew back, turning his face away.

What did they say afterwards?

Nothing. They were happy too. Sometimes they even asked me first.

Ernesto's eyes were drawn to a part of the man's body which was visibly aroused.

Let me see it, he said.

Happily. He was about to satisfy Ernesto's wish and his own, when the boy stopped him.

Let me take it out, he said. Can I?

Of course.

He bent down to act on his whim, but the man's shirt tails were so twisted around it that he needed help.

It's big, Ernesto said, half scared and half amused. Twice as big as mine.

Because you're still a boy. Wait till you're my age, then . . .

The boy put out his hand. The man stopped him.

No, not with your hand, else you'll make me come.

Isn't that what you want?

Yes, but not in your hand.

Ah! — Ernesto jerked his hand back as if from some forbidden thing. The man was edging nearer.

I'm scared, Ernesto said.

What of? Don't you know I love you?

I do believe you . . . but I'm scared you'll hurt me even so.

Me hurt you? I know how to treat a boy who's doing it for the first time, and you more than any other.

You won't put it all the way in, will you?

You're joking! Just the tip — hardly anything. The man smiled.

Well, you say that now . . . but when you're all stirred up . . .

How adorable you are! thought the man, and he vowed not to hurt the boy in any way, even if it meant less pleasure for himself.

I'd cut it off, he said, rather than hurt you. And he tried to kiss him, but as before Ernesto ducked aside.

Bend down now, *please*, the man begged. Time's passing and we're not getting anywhere.

So you want to get somewhere! Ernesto laughed.

You want to as well — that's why we're here, isn't it? As long, he added in a low quick voice, as long as you won't wish you hadn't later.

I've already told you I won't, but . . . but what

about a pledge?

What pledge? The man did not know what Ernesto meant. If he had not been poor and the boy (as *he* thought) well off, he would have expected a demand for money, and that would have spoiled everything.

You must swear to stop if I say so, whenever I say it.

I'm sure you won't need to say anything, but I promise all the same.

Promising's not enough: you've got to swear.

The man laughed. What d'you want me to swear by?

Don't laugh, give your word of honour. The boy held out his open hand as if to seal a contract.

The man took his hand. They shook.

Whenever you say and at once, the man swore.

Ernesto looked relieved.

Now . . . if you want to . . .

Bless you! Now take your jacket off (he had already removed his own) and your trousers too.

You as well.

Yes of course. The man began, then Ernesto had another whim.

Let me take yours off and you mine, he said. Can we?

The man agreed to everything.

Where do you want me to go?

Here — the man pointed to a low pile of sacks, with, at the top, the one whose label Ernesto had torn to shreds in his confusion. They were medium sized and marked with a double zero: the whitest, finest grade of all, superfine flour so costly that only a few bakers would buy it. The sacks were piled to a height which might have been arranged just for them, beneath an arch in a secret recess deep inside the warehouse, where they would never be found — if not by the eye of God.

Ernesto knelt by the sacks and leaned across them as his friend had asked. The man turned him round and slowly lifted up his shirt, which the boy, unconsciously teasing or, more likely, because of the anxiety spreading through him, had forgotten to take off. (The shirt was his last defence, the last barrier between him and the irrevocable.) The man was trembling as much as the boy.

He caressed the boy's body as he gradually laid it bare, but only for a moment, for he was afraid of making him impatient. So too he withheld the tender words raising from his heart: words full of gratitude and wonder, which (if he heard them at all) Ernesto would scarcely have appreciated. He said something coarse instead, as if in reply to those words the boy had just used, which had almost made him blush.

Ernesto said nothing back. Filled with curiosity and fear, he could not have said anything even had he wanted to. And for that matter, what was there to say? He heard the man softly asking him to shift position, and did so as if it was an order. All at once he thought *I'm lost*, but there was no regret, no wish to turn back. Then (and not at first without sweet pleasure) he felt a strange, unknown heat as the man found and made contact. Neither spoke, except for an *Angel!* that escaped the man just before he came, and a warning *Aah!* from the boy when he felt the man pressing too hard. But he kept his promise and did not hurt him in any way (or tried not to). In all it was easier and quicker than Ernesto had expected. As he withdrew from the boy the man asked him to stay as he was a moment longer. *What else can he want to do to me?* he wondered, but relaxed when he saw the man take a handkerchief out of his pocket; he only wanted to clean him (whether from kindness or to make sure he left no trace). It made Ernesto feel like a little baby. He felt bewildered and confused too, just as babies do.


You were good — good as gold, said the man when they were both dressed again and had brushed themselves down.

Ernesto frowned, but he was pleased by the man's praise.

Did you like it? he asked.

I was in heaven. But you liked it too — admit it.

Less than that! A bit at first, yes, then it hurt. I yelled as well.

You yelled?

Didn't you hear me yell *Aah!*? . . . And why did you call me an angel?

What else should I call you?

Angels don't do things like this, Ernesto said brusquely. They don't even have bodies.

We came together, said the man.

How d'you know?

I felt you coming — you can always feel it. And look down there . . .

Where? asked Ernesto, frightened now.

The man pointed to a dark patch on the sack of superfine flour which Ernesto had been bending over, the one with the shredded label.

The boy looked, and was mortified.

If you can see it we must turn the sack over. Don't you think we should?

Who could know what it is? asked the man. But I'll turn it over later if you still want me to.

There was a lingering, embarrassed silence. The man became thoughtful, almost louring.

Ernesto was rather alarmed. What are you thinking about? he asked.

I'm thinking there's something I must tell you and I

don't like having to say it. Maybe I should have said it before . . . You won't tell anyone what we've done, will you?

Who d'you think I might tell? I'm not that stupid — I know as well as you what you can say and what you can't.

The man looked relieved. But the worst still remained to say:

It's a dangerous thing, you know: people don't understand, and . . . and they can send you to prison for it.

I know that too, said Ernesto triumphantly. I read about a pair like us in the newspaper, a man and a boy caught red-handed in a changing room. The headline was WHAT HAPPENED AFTER A SWIM, and the boy got four months and the man six. That's ba-a-ad! he concluded, spinning out the *a* for no apparent reason.

And when you've done time, persisted the man, there's nothing left to do but drown yourself for shame. But he felt guilty at tormenting the boy so.

Don't worry, Ernesto said reassuringly, as long as we don't get caught like those two fools. It was the attendant who thought they'd gone, opened the door, found them doing it, and shouted the place down when he didn't need to say anything. Now *I* made sure you'd bolted the door before, though you didn't notice.

Ernesto smiled at the man, who was still pensive, even gloomy.

It's something else I'm thinking about, Ernesto added.

What's that? asked the man anxiously.

I'm wondering how I'll be able to look my mother in the face tonight.

As you do every other night, the man answered, hiding his dismay. If she doesn't know anything's happened nothing *has* happened.

*I* know that well enough, Ernesto said gravely. It'll be a problem going to the class too: she'll ask me on the way what I've been doing. My mother's very nosy, she always wants to know everything — everything that's happened during the day.

Women are always nosy but you still mustn't tell her anything at all, anything of what we've done, I mean. She'd forgive you perhaps, but never me . . . And don't think you're the only boy who's ever done what you just did. I asked you for love because I do love you. You're not like other boys, who do it once and never want to see you again. You *are* like an angel to me, and that's another reason I don't want any harm to come your way from this.

All right, said Ernesto. Then after a pause:

How many boys do you think have done it? — what I've done today?

What do you mean, how many boys?

Well, out of a hundred, say, how many . . .?

How do I know? The man laughed uneasily. All I can say is, I never asked a boy who said no.

This was true; what he did not add was that, guided by a nearly infallible sixth sense, he only ever approached boys who had this particular curiosity in their adolescence. (They nearly all changed later and forgot the whole affair — or tried to.) And (while the man could not have told Ernesto this, at least not yet) many gave themselves for cash. Their price was only a florin — not much, but day-labourers did not always have a florin to spend as they liked. If he had been well off he would have given Ernesto a splendid present (not money), both in gratitude for past pleasure and because he knew how much boys love presents — nothing thrills them more. But he couldn't have done it even with the money in his pocket: the boy would have been bound to show his mother or his friends (for some reason the man was sure Ernesto had lots of friends, whereas he had very few at this time, if any); he could not have kept it hidden if he had wanted to. He would have bought him a gold tie-pin, studded with a tiny precious stone, perhaps, in the fashion of the day. But thinking about it was all he could do.

Ernesto, meanwhile, was walking restlessly about the warehouse, looking nervous. The man had taken out his needle and thread and set to work.

We must get down to it, he said, or the boss will make all sorts of fuss when he comes in.

Ernesto sat down beside him and watched him sew but did not sit still for long. He was soon back on his feet, pacing to and fro . . .

What are you touching yourself for?

I'm burning hot, Ernesto said apologetically, as if he was to blame.

Don't worry, the man said gently, it's nothing, it'll pass in an hour, probably much sooner.

Sure?

Certain. I was so careful, I can't think why you feel anything now.

Can I ask you something?

Of course you can.

Is it true they examine you there at the army medical and throw out anyone who . . .

The man burst out laughing, but this time too there was something forced in his laughter. He reassured the boy about this question, as he had done before; he had been conscripted himself eight years ago and no one had even thought of examining him in the place Ernesto was worried about. Not him or anybody else.

Who the devil put that stupid idea into your head?

No one put it into my head, Ernesto replied, some-what piqued. (Did the man take him for an idiot?)

Someone I know once told me. Last year.

The man remembered he had once heard something similar himself, and believed it too at first. But Ernesto was an educated person: how could he credit such a silly tale? He realized that the boy was remorseful, at least for the moment, and wanted comforting; that all these notions and complaints — even these smartings — were more the effect of his remorse than anything else. He in his hard egoism hoped it would prove to be a passing mood; quite apart from his love for the boy — itself rare enough in a man like him — he felt none of the revulsion he had always experienced with other boys, whom he left — fled from, indeed — as soon as he had possessed them. It seemed to him he could have stayed with Ernesto for ever, and even if he *had* had to scare the boy a little, he was upset to see him worried and downcast.

Are you still thinking about your mother?

No, not now.

Of what then?

. . . Nothing.

The man set to work again but soon stopped to ask, in an almost motherly way:

Does it still hurt?

Yes, still. This time the boy's voice was reproachful.

Another time, ventured the man, I'll bring something that'll stop any pain, during or after.

Ernesto was intrigued. What is it?

Something you buy at the chemist's.

You mean the chemist sells something for *this*? Well . . .

No, not for that, the man said, it's for people with tummy upsets. It's a cone you put up there and five minutes later all the burning is gone. Then you wouldn't feel any of what you say is hurting you now.

What's the cone made of?

Cocoa butter, answered the man, with no idea of the effect his words would have.

Cocoa butter — cocoa butter! Ernesto chanted the words over and over until he dissolved into laughter, and laughed so hard that he had to sit down, tears running down his cheeks. He looked as if he could never stop.

Cocoa butter — up your arse! You know it all, you do! He laughed so delightedly and long that his fresh, young high spirits cleared away the clouding heaviness from the room. The man joined in the laughter and seemed happy and relaxed by his boy's jubilation as he sang the ingredient of his medicine and the way it needs to be applied. The man was longing to hug Ernesto and kiss him, but he was not brave enough to try; experience had taught him that boys don't like kisses — don't know how to give or accept them. He looked thankfully, tenderly, at the boy, and at the same moment heard someone hammering on the door almost angrily. It was the boss, who had been knocking for some time, now grown impatient when nobody let him in. He was thinking that neither Ernesto nor the hired man had even showed up: they had forgotten his orders of the afternoon before — disobeyed him. Ernesto was still laughing too much to stand up and go to the door, so he gave the keys to the man, who hurried to let the boss in. He entered grim-faced, glancing around suspiciously, and asked Ernesto in his usual vile Italian what there was to be so jolly about. Ernesto (who always preferred not to say anything when he could not tell the truth) was at a loss for words. The boss shrugged and kept looking at his young apprentice, but not in anger; he liked the boy, though he was too afraid of losing face ever to let him know it. He muttered a *verfluchte Kerl* (bloody boy) and stepped over to his office, instructing Ernesto to be with him in (glancing at the clock) five minutes' time. He had to give him and the workman their orders for the afternoon's delivery.


Aren't you going to turn the sack over? Ernesto asked, calm at last and remembering what had worried him before.

Straightaway, but not because we need to, believe me. It's only another bit of work. But for your peace of mind — he looked lovingly at the boy — I'll gladly do it.

## Second Episode

Ernesto didn't like the man to call him *tu*. He did not always use it, to be sure — only a few times, when they were by themselves. Yet they were safely alone together more often now than before: the very circumstances at work encouraged an intimacy which was beginning to weary Ernesto if not, yet, to annoy him. Perhaps the poor boy had not found the element of paternal protection he was unconsciously seeking; for he was younger than his years and effectively fatherless (the guardian uncle only counted for the clouting and the weekly florins). He complained about the *tu* after they had buttoned up their clothes one day.

When you're with a kid, came the answer, you're bound to call him *tu* once in a while. But it's only a little thing — you're not offended, are you?

No, no offence, but the cat's out of the bag if you make a habit of it, then let slip a *tu* when anybody else is near. (Some of the fear of discovery seemed to have passed from the man to the boy; the man was still too besotted for fear to get the better of him.)

The experiment with the cone was not a success. The man brought it with him one day wrapped in silver foil, so that Ernesto was reminded of almond cake, which in turn reminded him of Christmas. He put Ernesto (who looked sceptical) in a suitable position (the same position the man possessed him in), bending over the usual pile of sacks, which had not yet found a buyer so were still stacked under the arch. Then he pushed in the cone as deep as possible, ig-

noring the boy's protests and telling him not to move
for five minutes. But at the end Ernesto felt just the
same, and at his entreaty the man satisfied him with his
hand. Ernesto could see he was reluctant to do it,
which spoiled the keen physical pleasure.

I'm fed up, he announced another time. Can't I do it
myself once?

The man had been expecting this, and fearing it too.
On one hand he was frightened of women; on the
other he would prefer Ernesto to find relief with a boy
his own age. It would have seemed less sinful, less
harmful.

Who with?

Why not with you? He looked at the man, but
without much conviction.

The man laughed, and Ernesto thought his laughter
was horrid; but it was only embarrassment.

It isn't good doing it to a man, he said. It's something you only do to boys before they start shaving,
and — he was about to add *before they start going with
women*, but stopped himself in time. — How could you
want me with this moustache of mine? (he smoothed it
as he spoke.) If I was a lad your own age I'd gladly
take it in turn with you.

Couldn't you shave it off? asked Ernesto, knowing
it was nonsense before he spoke.

That wouldn't be any use, I'd be a man just the same.

Ernesto did not come to the office next day, nor for
the rest of the week. The man did not know what to
make of his absence, and dared not ask the only person
who could have given him any news — Signor Wilder.
In the event it was he who told him, without the man
having to say a word. He was rummaging through all
the drawers in Ernesto's desk, searching for bills; they
should have been there but all he found was a complete
mess, with a number of books from the Biblioteca

Economica Sonzogno series (Wilder the businessman glanced contemptuously at the titles) and in a heap of other papers a caricature which, luckily for Ernesto, Signor Wilder (who liked and understood only one of the arts: music, meaning *German* music) did not recognize. It was one of Ernesto's tasks to collect payment on the invoices from the bakers in the city and suburbs, but, always taking no for an answer, he was not a good debt-collector, and a debtor only needed to show the least degree of reluctance for Ernesto to say he would call back in a week's time. So, quite apart from reaping the blessings of embarrassed customers he could look forward to another walk around the city — and to the wrath of Signor Wilder, which never failed to ensue on these occasions. It was the bills and invoices he was thinking of now; he thought the *verfluchte Kerl* (as he privately called Ernesto, for whom at the same time he felt none of the antipathy or suspicion which all his other employees aroused in him) must have left them in his jacket pocket. He called the man and told him to go to Ernesto's house straightaway — he was ill in bed — and find out where he had hidden those damned bills and bring them back if they were still in his possession. The man blushed as he listened to Signor Wilder. He would have been delighted to see Ernesto again, and his home for the first time, if not for fear of meeting his mother, for it was on *her* account (not the boy's) that he felt guilty. He did not ask about Ernesto's illness — being sure it was nothing serious — and walked slowly and rather reluctantly to his house. He already knew the address which the boss had told him in the course of his instructions, then written on a postcard, just to be safe.

The door was opened by a rather stout, stooping

woman, bent not so much by age as by illness or suffering. At first glance one would never have guessed she was Ernesto's mother, for the boy was slenderly built; never have thought that one form had produced the other. Yet an observer less preoccupied than the man was at that moment, would soon have recognized the son's eyes in the colour and shape of the mother's, and found a distant but quite unmistakable resemblance in every line of her face; and despite his embarrassment the man knew this was the mother. She held the door ajar, as if she could not decide whether she should open it to this stranger — for what could he want? She thought he must have the wrong floor, or the wrong door at least.

Whom do you want?

The boss sent me, I've got to speak to Signor Ernesto about some papers they need at the office.

My son hasn't been well. He's still in bed but he's much better already. I'll go and tell him you're here and what it is Signor Wilder wants. Please . . .

She opened the door. The man followed her into the room.

I know who you are, the woman went on, my son often talks about you. I'll be back in a moment. And she went to announce Ernesto's unexpected visitor.

The man knew by her tone of voice that if Ernesto had told his mother about him, nothing compromising had passed his lips. This thought, or certainty rather, revived him. He probably told her a few harmless bits of gossip (as much to satisfy her curiosity as anything else), he thought, or blamed the boss for being mean in his dealings with me. What a fine boy Ernesto is — what a treasure! He felt how much he owed the boy, not only for what they did together but for the way he knew how to do it and not talk about it. The mother was gone a long time. Although he was only a common labourer, a member of the 'servant class' (the year, remember, is 1898, and the place Trieste), Signora Celestina may have wanted to tidy her son's room a little before introducing their visitor.

Oh do let him in, he heard Ernesto shout irritably. The boy was apparently not very interested in the mere tidiness of his room and wanted to know without more ado what the man had come to say.

The small brass bedstead was set against the wall halfway across the room. The roof sloped towards the window. There was a bird cage — a big one, at Ernesto's insistence — by the window, with a blackbird singing as it perched one-legged on the highest bar. Everything in the little room had an old-fashioned, almost antique flavour, certainly closer to the beginning than to the end of the century.

The boy was not wearing a shirt, perhaps because of the early hot weather that year, and he looked a little thinner than before. His mother had pleaded with him to put one on for the stranger, but in vain, and he wore nothing above the blankets but a vest. He sat up when the man entered and folded his hands behind his head. There were two little tufts in his armpits.

When greetings had been exchanged the man took the offered seat by the foot of the bed and asked after Ernesto's health. His mother wanted to give details of the illness and all the symptoms, but the boy interrupted and wouldn't let her finish. (In sum: he had had very bad stomach aches, and ran such a high temperature for a day or two that they were terrified he might have typhoid, but the doctor reassured her at once — he was an old semi-retired practitioner who had attended at Ernesto's birth, and his mother trusted him implicitly. Now he was on the mend — all but recovered — and longing above all to be out of bed.)

What does the old man want?

He can't find the week's bills, the man said, and he sent me to see if they're in your jacket pocket or if you know where they can be in the office. He's been through all your drawers, he couldn't find a single one.

Ernesto had almost forgotten the caricature, and felt no pangs of conscience where his employer (or rather his *exploiter*, as he learned to call him when he started reading *The Worker*, despite his guardian uncle's prohibition) was concerned, and he told the man yes, he did still have them. He asked his mother to hand him his jacket, which was neatly folded (and not by his hands) over the arm of a settee. She did so, and the boy took a little bundle of bills from one of the pockets.

Here, he said, give these to the old scrooge.

I don't know why my son always says such wicked things about good Signor Wilder, the woman said, turning to the man. I hope that you don't encourage him anyway.

The man could not think what to say.

My mother's on the bosses' side too, Ernesto said. Then, because he really did want to offer his friend something or wished to be alone with him for a moment, he told his mother to bring the man a glass of wine.

The man hesitated but Ernesto insisted, and practically ordered his mother to hurry up about it.

She obeyed.

How hard you are on your mother! said the man as soon as she had shut the door. That's the last thing I expected after what you told me.

I do love her but she's too nosy: she always wants to stay and hear everything . . . Can you see Pimpo?

Pimpo?

My blackbird Pimpo, there in the window.

The man turned to where Ernesto was pointing. He looked at the bird.

Does it sing?

Too much! We have to cover the cage with a black cloth at night or the whole house is woken up before dawn . . . I've got a hen as well.

In a kitchen coop?

No, not in a coop, I like having her free in the kitchen, at least when I'm at home. I let the blackbird out too, every day nearly. It has a bath in a big bowl here in the middle of my room. It's the only room with a sloping roof but I like it. I'm happy in here.

What does your mother say?

What, about the sloping roof?

About the animals.

Sometimes she grumbles, other times she doesn't mind. She's almost glad about the hen because of the eggs, which she gives me in hot drinks. She thinks they're better for me new-laid. I used to like them too but not now so much, the same as cod-liver oil . . .

You used to *like* that cod oil stuff? the man asked incredulously.

I pretended to when I was a kid for my mother's sake and because I wanted her to be pleased with me. I don't like it nowadays, though my mother still chases me waving the bottle, with the doctor egging her on. I know it would make me sick. What's the news at work?

Nothing I know of, said the man, except — adding this in a low voice — I miss you all the time.

I'm better now, Ernesto said, and I'm getting up tomorrow morning whether my mother wants me to or not. I'll have a bath, put all clean clothes on, then off to work straight after breakfast, purged, changed and clean, and — he added, also in a low voice — you can do what you want to me, but . . .

His mother came in with a plate in her hand, and on the plate a brimming glass of red wine. Although he did not much care for wine (unlike his mate Cesco) the man took the glass with thanks, toasted their good health, emptied it at a draught and wiped his moustache with the back of his hand. In other words he behaved just as Ernesto, and still more Ernesto's mother, expected a man of his class to behave. Then he excused himself — the boss was waiting for the papers — and rose to take his leave. For different reasons neither of the others offered a hand, and he was already at the door when Ernesto, sitting bolt upright now, waved his arms above his head and shouted, cried out as he laughed (like someone bursting with pent-up words): . . . but no more CONES!

The man wanted the earth to swallow him up. The mother was certain — as good as certain — to ask her son the meaning of that strange shout as soon as he was out of the house, and Ernesto (who did not know how to lie) would have to lie to answer at all. But the mother did not give it a second thought; she was a thousand miles from imagining the perfidy (if perfidy it was) which inspired it. She thought the cone was a reference to something at the office — some gossip or other, probably about their miserly employer. The man did not sleep a wink all night, while Ernesto slept sweetly and awoke the next morning fully recovered, more than ready to return to normal life. He had almost forgotten the terror he had struck — God alone knows why! — into the man's heart, for fun.

Ernesto could not bear anyone to be angry with him for long. Always quick to forgive, he wanted quick forgiveness for himself as well. But after a dreadful night and an anxious morning the man was impatient to see him, both for his own present peace of mind and to scold the one who had so rudely shattered it the day before.

The boy was punctual as ever. He arrived in high spirits with the big warehouse keys ready in his hand, as if in a hurry to open up. He looked revitalized by his short illness and softened by the hot bath, in which he had lingered luxuriously. Through his worry and anger the man knew that he loved him — loved him too much. Yet there was a shade of sadism in his love, and it was this which sought expression under cover of the shout. It went badly for him, as we shall see.

How many do you think you deserve? he asked, barely convinced by the boy's assurance that his mother had neither understood nor suspected a thing.

How many what?

How many strokes with a birch wand? He was unbuttoning Ernesto's trousers, following their ritual, while the boy stood still, arms hanging by his sides.

I thought you meant cakes, he said. (The man sometimes brought a few cakes with him, being the only presents he could afford and the only ones which . . . left no trace. Ernesto was not one to stand on ceremony — he always devoured them on the spot.)

Why do you want to beat me when I've only given you what you liked?

As a little punishment.

So it's little, is it? If I was wrong to do what we did you're hardly the one to punish me now.

I don't need to tell you that's not the reason.

What then? Because I shouted about the cones?

That too, but that's not all. You're too handsome — tease me too much — think it's a joke making me go out of my mind.

Ernesto was aggrieved at being called a tease. He did not think he was at all handsome; he never looked at himself in the mirror. And if he did tease him it was unintentional.

The man could not help himself: he smacked
Ernesto on the part of his body which he had just laid
bare. It did not hurt, but the man's five fingers were
marked in blushing outline on Ernesto's flesh.

Stop there, he said crossly, covering the place with
his hand. It was warm to the touch. When he saw the
man prolonging the usual caresses, as if to show his
contrition, he said Come on, do it.

The man's pleasure that day was more intense than
any he could remember in his life, but Ernesto was
bored and decided this was the last time. When they
were dressed again the man went out for a few minutes
and returned with a bag of 'fourpenny tarts': three
pastry horns oozing yellow custard, costing four *soldi*
each. These were Ernesto's favourite cakes, and he did
not object when he saw them now. Out of courtesy he
offered one to the man, who refused, as always, and
Ernesto ate all three. Then he sat beside the man on the
usual stacks of flour. Neither wanted to start work; the
labourer had no more wish to mend torn sacks than
Ernesto had to move into the little room which served
as his office, next to the boss's study, where there was
almost a week's work waiting for him.

A penny for your thoughts, said the man.

Ernesto laughed. I'm thinking about the old man, he
said.

Never mind him.

I can't understand . . ., Ernesto began. Although he
had made up his mind not to comply any more with
the man's desires, he bore him no ill-will and still
enjoyed their conversations. When he came to read the
*Iliad* in the Monti translation for the first, entrancing
time, he would imagine Ulysses as being physically
like the man. And for that matter, if he had been of the
same class as the boy — the same spiritual class at least
— instead of a poor day-labourer; if in other words he

could have educated him, helped bring him to self-knowledge, the rewards would not have been all on one side and the relationship might have lasted longer. But as it was . . .

I can't think why he puts up with me and doesn't throw me out (which is just what I want, by the way). You don't know half the rotten things I do . . .

What things? The man was shaken by this openly avowed wish to be dismissed by Signor Wilder. Knowing nothing of the boy's new decision, he was already wondering where in that case they could meet. Outside the city perhaps, in the evening? But the boy couldn't or wouldn't meet after work, and anyway where could be better than here in the warehouse? Ernesto is always right, he thought, remembering who had first suggested this place. He had loaded and unloaded all Signor Wilder's carts for little enough pay simply to be near the boy.

The boss can't stand the smell of naphthalene, he says it gives him headaches. So I put it in all the corners and under the furniture too. Then he grumbles and goes out for a walk — to find some air, as he puts it. He thinks it's the cleaning woman, so next morning he yells at her: she uses far too much of the stuff and never opens the windows beforehand. But that's not all I do, oh no!

What else? As usual the man was hugely entertained by Ernesto's chatter, though he suspected some of his stories were invented, or at least exaggerated.

Lots of things, Ernesto said. For one, you don't know it but he often writes four- or five-page letters — in German, because I write the Italian ones. It's not done to write such long letters in business, but him . . . he's manic, specially when he's writing to Louisen-Muhle (Luigia Mills), his main supplier; he takes a whole afternoon to write them one letter. By about five o'clock he's had enough and goes out for a coffee. So I lick my fingers and make a big smear on the first or second page, which looks like an ink smudge. He sees it when he comes back, swears like a Turk and has to copy the whole thing out again, while I'm in stitches next door!

Hasn't he ever caught on? asked the man disbelievingly.

Never. He never says anything anyway. And then he can't stand little street-kids (the same ones you like too much): they're as bad as naphthalene. So I pay them (he really did, but not in cash: with stamps cut off the envelopes, which the urchins used as currency) to chase each other in through one door and out of the other. (The office's two doors gave on to different streets.) The boss charges out right on cue and wants me to chase after them. The old fool doesn't see I'm behind it in the first place. He threatens to call the police, but it's not the police he needs! But there's an even better trick I thought of myself one day.

The man enjoyed listening but was still sceptical. He did not know — could not bring himself to believe — that Ernesto was telling the strict truth; for Ernesto was such an upright boy . . . Then he remembered that shout about the cones and was more inclined to believe him.

What was it you thought of?

Thought of and carried out! Did you ever notice that pair of canary-coloured gloves he wore all the time till recently? — till just before we . . . They irritated me so much, because of the colour and a bit because of the way he used to pull them on . . . They were revolting. Well, I made plans with another boy who lives near here (an old mate from school) and bought some bunches of tamarind. Well as you know tamarind is the same colour as — as something else, and before opening the office I wiped both door handles with it. As soon as I saw the boss come to open his door I came in by the other. Then I sniffed and smelled my hand, making sure he saw me, and yelled *Shit! It's shit! The little bastards wiped shit on the door handles!* The old man's eyes flew to his gloves — all stained. How was he to know it was only tamarind? He couldn't work out what had happened! And he very, very nearly found me out. He tore the gloves off and threw them in the bin, mean as he is, though I think he fished them out later and had them cleaned. He hasn't worn them since, or if he has I haven't seen them.

The man laughed, enjoying himself more than ever.

But the story of the lamps is the best of all. One wonderful afternoon last winter I bought a little box of those caps that kids fire in toy pistols (I think they're called *amorfi*). They make a little bang, nothing bad, and don't cost much. I put one under the mantle of his desk lamp to see what happened when he lit the gas. There was a little bang and the mantle was wrecked, not surprisingly. So he swore and sent for another straightaway, as he never buys more than one at a time. Meanwhile I put another cap in my own lamp, so that went out of action too. Then he blew his top with the people who sell the mantles. He said they did it on purpose to sell more, of course I backed him up for all I was worth and pretended to be angry too: I agreed that mantle-sellers are thieves to a man. Luck was on my side all the way, because the man who went to buy a new mantle (you haven't met him yet) came back empty-handed: the shop was out of stock. We could only get more by going a long way and waiting Lord knows how long, but the boss wanted to finish the letter he'd started to his Louisen-Muhle and had had all he could take. He sent the man home to borrow a petrol lamp from his wife while he went out for a coffee, as always, and to have a read of his national newspapers, because he never reads the *Piccolo*, it's always the *Frankfurter Zeitung* or something like that — I saw him reading it once when I went to fetch him at the café when a mill owner arrived out of the blue and wanted to speak to him in a hurry. That wonderful afternoon, just before he came back (I was keeping watch behind a door) I dunked the glass lampshade in a bucket of water and of course the glass cracked as well. He wasn't even upset — didn't have the strength; he bowed to fate. And the idiot still doesn't see that *I'm* his fate.

See how much you deserve the spanking, said the man tenderly.

Forget the spanking, that's only for babies. What *I* still want to know is why he hasn't grasped who's behind all this.

He's in love with you, said the man, quick to discover his own proclivity in other people, and pretending not to know so he doesn't have to sack you.

Ernesto pulled a disgusted face.

You shouldn't think I do what I do with you with anybody else. Besides he's old (in fact he was not old at all, but in Ernesto's eyes all men and women over thirty-five were old, indeed ripe for the grave) and married. Haven't you seen how beautiful his wife is? She's got a moustache — almost like yours.

Then I can't believe he's never cottoned on who's plaguing him.

It isn't only he's never cottoned on: he even gave me a cane with a silver knob when we met in the street one day — he was actually carrying it at the time. I didn't know what to say. Well, of course I said thank you — what else could I do? — just as if I was pleased with his present.

The man was very surprised.

SECOND EPISODE · 45

Don't you like getting presents?

I love it, but what does he expect me to do with a
silver-knobbed cane? I'm not an old man or a dandy, I
never carry one. So it stays at home for my mother to
guard like a medal — proof of the glory her son has
won . . . If only she knew!

Knew what?

These terrible things I do to my boss! Or did, rather;
I lost the urge a while ago. He's too stupid, it's not even
any fun making him lose his temper.

A light veil of sadness had fallen over Ernesto's
childish face after so much laughter. And I'll be
seventeen in a few days, he added. I'm getting on and
soon have to start thinking how to keep my mother
and me. And it's my nanny's birthday the day after
tomorrow, I need to think what to give her.

So you've a nanny too?

Certainly I do, and I love her. I'm not the only one to
love his nanny, there's a great poet who is still alive and
he had a nanny too. His name's d'Annunzio. He must
be an old man now but he's written a long poem for her
all the same. It's called *Alla mia nutrice* (*To my Nurse*). A
cousin of mine sent me a copy from wherever they
printed the book. It's very beautiful — well I like it a lot
anyway, I almost know it by heart.

There was a short silence. The man did not know
what to say; he looked frightened — and he was.

I don't know if I ever told you, Ernesto went on,
that I lived with my nanny in her house in the country
till I was four or five. First my mother lost her milk
because of all her sorrows. Then she owned a little
furniture business, so she had no time for me. She says
she's never had a moment's happiness since I came into
the world. She was often sick, so she was glad she
could leave me with my nanny.

What do you want to give her?

Half a kilo of coffee and a kilo of sugar, Ernesto answered, for he was a practical as well as a serious boy. She's poor and I think those will be useful. But I don't know that I have enough money.

(How gladly the man would have offered him some money! But he would not have dared even if he had been able, for the boy might have taken offence — might have thought the money was proffered in exchange for his consent.)

You made me think of my nanny, Ernesto continued, when you told me what I deserved for that shout and the tricks I liked playing and I said that's only for babies.

Did your nanny beat you?

I can't remember, not properly. But she says she sometimes did, and hard too. She says she always relented when I started to cry. Maybe I did deserve it from my nanny, but certainly not from you. And he looked at the man severely.

During this exchange the man had got up and hurriedly unbolted the warehouse door. It was time to open, and he did not want the boss or anyone else to find them locked inside and alone. It was unlikely that anyone would think twice, but the man's conscience was not clear and he was always nervous, more or less.


I've brought it with me, the man said the next day.

What's that? asked Ernesto without much interest.

The birch.

What for?

For you, ventured the man slyly.

Ernesto's eyes widened.

Show me, he said.

The man took the birch wand from behind a sack and showed the boy. He had just come by way of the

Boschetto, where he had selected this particular wand with loving care. Freshly cut and whippy, it would sting bare flesh like the devil.

Give it to me.

Only if you promise to give it back.

I'm not promising anything. I said give it to me.

Humbled by the boy's imperious tone, the man gave him the wand.

Now your hand, Ernesto said, like this — and he held the man's left hand open, as schoolmasters do in junior school when they catch someone not paying attention and want to punish him.

Again the man obeyed. Ernesto took his hand by the fingertips and held it open and steady. He flexed the birch wand to and fro (as if to test it) and let fly a cruel lash. The man's face twisted with pain and his hand flew back as if scalded. He shook his hand about, to cool it on the air.

Ernesto laughed.

How many did you want to give me? he asked.

Five, came the ingenuous answer.

Ernesto reached both hands behind to touch his buttocks, and he rubbed them as if they really had been beaten.

You've been totting up the bill without the landlord, he said, remembering a not inappropriate expression he often heard his uncle use. Still laughing, he broke the birch wand into little pieces and threw them away, just as once, their first afternoon, he had thrown away the shreds of the label from the sack of superfine flour.

Now let's work, he said briskly, like someone addressing a subordinate. But when he realized how dejected the man was he added more kindly:

Forgive me for hurting you. I only wanted to play, just as you wanted to play, I know (he did not know this at all — was sure in fact the opposite was true). If there is still a bit of pain, remember it was me, Ernesto, who did it to you. Then it won't hurt so much.

## Third Episode

It's time you had a haircut, his mother told Ernesto one morning. I don't want to see you looking like that any longer — here's some money, do go and see Bernardo on your way back for lunch.

Bernardo was a barber with a shop across the street from Ernesto's house.

Signora Celestina had been asking Ernesto to undergo this little operation for more than a month. She was devoted to tidiness and could not bear her son going about like a savage or an orphan in a storm; but Ernesto never liked to lose any part of himself, even when the part always grew back. When he was a tiny boy in his nanny's house, one reason why she used to beat him was his resistance to having his nails cut; as the dreadful moment approached and he saw her fetch the scissors, he — who freely submitted to her other commands — dashed here and there around the bed-room, finally diving under the bed. He was as precious to her as her own son (who had died in infancy) would have been, but it was no easy task to prise him out of his bolt-hole, and she had all the other household things to do as well, so she sometimes lost patience.

Bernardo? Do you mean my father? said Ernesto.

If I ever hear that lie out of you again I'll tell your uncle Giovanni, Signora Celestina replied (as always). He'll teach you a thing or two — he'll make you respect your mother. Then (as always) she burst into tears.

It was an old slander. When she had owned a little

furniture shop near Bernardo the barber's, they used to pass the time chatting from their doorsteps when work was slack. That was all. But the street was full of gossips, and what with Signora Celestina's strange marriage, so quickly followed by legal separation (for reasons still unknown . . .), those chats about the weather did the rest. Two years before this story starts, a cousin of Ernesto's own age had explained how babies are made and born (matters about which he had only had the haziest idea before), then went on to tell him almost as a corollary that everyone at home knew Bernardo was Ernesto's real father, and this was the reason (never to be whispered abroad!) for his parents' (so-called, in one case) separation. Thrilled at discovering the mysteries of procreation and by his secret kinship with Bernardo, he ran home all bright and excited to tell his mother both bits of news. At the first her face fell, and she opened her mouth to denounce his corrupting cousin; at the second, she fainted clean away. Ernesto was stricken with remorse (already seeing his mother dead, killed by the shock) and did not know what to do; he could have throttled the blackbird, which trilled all unaware in the window: surely its song had never rung so clear and fine! A pinch of bromide set things right for the moment, but whenever his mother urged him to go to the barber (which happened two or three times a year) he took revenge by repeating the old line, though by now he knew it was slander pure and simple. His mother was hurt and angry every time and always threatened to punish him by telling uncle Giovanni. For his part, beside the fact that he knew his mother's threats were hollow, Ernesto could see nothing wrong with being Bernardo's son.

The barber was a large, kind-faced man, white haired and well past middle age. He always gave

Ernesto a warm welcome — had once even lent him a few pennies (which the boy punctually repaid from his guardian uncle's weekly hand-out) to squander in a new cake shop that was the talk of Trieste. He had known Ernesto and been tending him since he was a tiny boy, for he was the first to cut his hair after his nanny, and looked forward now to trimming his first beard. Bernardo predicted a brilliant future for the boy; according to him he was destined come what may to be rich one day, thanks to some sort of legacy which would be his as if by right. The first blow to his hopes came with the day Ernesto left school to start work; he obviously belonged to that very substantial category of people who cannot imagine a brilliant career not being prefaced by a university degree. He never mentioned his disappointment to Ernesto, who sensed it none the less. He could have gone to a different barber, but that would have seemed a petty betrayal of someone who had always treated him kindly and affectionately. For this reason, and not to have to endure his mother's reproaches over lunch, he went for the haircut that morning; and stepped resolutely into the shop.

Bernardo wanted this customer for himself; he took the towel from his assistant as he was about to tuck it into the boy's collar, asked for the scissors and set to work. Once settled in the swivel chair, totally in the power of his unwitting tormentor, Ernesto resigned himself to the haircut as one of sweet life's necessities, however nasty it might be (years later, when life had turned hostile and grown difficult for him, he would call it not sweet but *passionate*). He only asked Bernardo not to cut too close, then cheerfully answered all his questions.

Knowing Ernesto had been ill and making sure he knew that he knew, the barber first asked after his health and after his mother and the aged aunt. Then he described how uncle Giovanni had called in the day before to have his beard trimmed. (He seemed proud of this.) His uncle had talked about him and complained that he was still a socialist: Everyone hates socialists, he'd said, how can they hope to get on in the world?

Is that true, what your uncle says about you? asked Bernardo.

(Sometimes Bernardo used *lei* with him and sometimes *tu*. He began using *lei* when Ernesto first came into his shop wearing long trousers, though he lapsed now and then into his old familiarity. Ernesto had known the barber for as long as he could remember, and he preferred *tu*.)

I'm still a socialist, yes, but I haven't joined the party yet, I'm still too young. The socialists are right but I'd be on their side even if they weren't, because it would annoy uncle Giovanni.

Bernardo knew Ernesto well enough not to take his words too seriously, and he laughed. He knew the boy did not hate his uncle (he didn't hate anybody yet): he was simply afraid of him, felt that he did not love him (or not much) and disapproved of him still more. (Perhaps he sensed something wayward and forbidden in his nephew.) And the need for love and approval went deep in Ernesto's character.

He tells me you're a poet as well. Is that true too?

The boy blushed.

My uncle's crazy, he said. He's probably seen me reading a book of poems and just assumed I must be a poet too.

And you still play the violin, Bernardo said, touching another tender spot. I can hear you from here. I always say to Giacomino (the assistant), There's our Ernesto practising the violin.

Ernesto was on tenterhooks for praise: would have

given anything for it, though he knew very well he did not deserve any. Learning the violin had been his own idea, a fancy with which he had persevered. It started when a famous Bohemian virtuoso was performing in Trieste and, hearing talk of violins and violinists, Ernesto (who was fifteen at the time) had sold his stamp album without telling a soul and bought a violin by adding a few crowns of his own to the five gained by the sale. He paid the teacher himself with the weekly florin he was already getting from his uncle, and some little subsidies wrung from his old aunt with promises and cajolery. He had no ear for music, but anyway it was too late to learn an instrument — at least everyone said so — for one needs to start in earliest childhood. When she saw him come home with a violin under his arm, his mother shrugged and compressed her disapproval into a curt phrase; Ernesto felt this was a bad omen. Then there was his uncle, who hated all violins on principle and his nephew's in particular. He said there had only been one real violinist — Paganini — and when he wanted to make Ernesto despair he laughed and called him 'our budding Paganini'. (The irony vested in these words hurt the boy more than any slaps around the head.) The old aunt was the only person who did not completely disapprove of the attempt; she said that patience and willpower can solve any problem, even a good ear can be acquired with training and one day he might be able to play in an orchestra and earn something to supplement his proper salary. But the aunt was a bit deaf as well as old, and the only work Signora Celestina let her do was clean the chicory, which everyone in the household was very partial to. The boy meanwhile was determined to persevere with his beloved/hated violin, however meagre the results; sometimes he dreamed of being a concert violinist himself, emulating the famous Bohemian whose triumphs he still read about in the newspapers and who was responsible for 'that kids' fad' (to quote the uncle). On this score Ernesto was adamant, and being such a chatterbox, it was almost incredible that he had never mentioned it to the man.

Now he wanted Bernardo to hurry up and finish, but the barber showed no sign of haste: he almost seemed to enjoy taking as long as possible over what for Ernesto was sheer torture, and who can say — who will ever know — if Bernardo's small-talk, humming in the boy's ears as he brushed his hair with special care, did not briefly transform him into a son of his own?

Your uncle can't stand socialists, he said, he earns too much himself; besides he was all for Garibaldi when he was young.

If Garibaldi was alive today, Ernesto retorted, he'd be a socialist. The line was not his own: he had liked it when he read it in *The Worker* recently, so he appropriated it. Bernardo did not want to keep contradicting him, and anyway he was almost finished. When the job appeared to be done he put a mirror into his young customer's hands to judge and pronounce his satisfaction. Ernesto glanced sidelong at his reflection and shut his eyes at the sight of himself so disfigured (as he thought). His neck felt unpleasantly chilly where Bernardo had used the razor.

Grand, he said, thank you. And he was already half out of the chair (apart from anything else he was ravenous) when Bernardo brushed his cheek with the back of his hand.

Just a moment, he said, there's a bit of beard here. If you can wait I'll have it off in a trice.

Ernesto did not have the nerve to object. There was not really any beard — only a light down which could very well have stayed where it was on the boy's as-yet-unshaven face. His instinct was to jump up and run away but diffidence apart, he would have had to explain why, and there was either nothing *to* say or nothing he *could* say. For a second he seemed to see the man far off, weeping. In the meantime, unaware of his customer's turmoil, Bernardo had already lathered his cheeks and was very slowly, very carefully grazing the blade over them. It was his trade, after all, and if there had been no beards Bernardo would surely have invented them himself.

At last Ernesto was free to stand and go. No one noticed the tears in his eyes. He thanked the barber again and left, forgetting — as he had never done before — to pay. Bernardo smiled happily as he folded the towel and watched Ernesto flee for home. Still hoping for a tip, Giacomino commented on the boy's forgetfulness, but the barber had no intention of calling him back.

He can always pay another time, he said, and if he doesn't, he doesn't.

A soft breeze lifting off the sea sharpened the chill on Ernesto's neck and face. He felt stripped, naked, and could not wait to be home again. He hoped his mother would realize how much he needed comforting, though he knew the hope was vain.

Mother, Bernardo made me have a proper shave, he said in a voice full of catastrophe, as soon as she opened the door. She did not understand her son's anguish, nor did it even occur to her to give him so much as a word of welcome, let alone kiss the cheek which had just felt a razor for the first time.

You're at the age when young men start growing beards, she said; Bernardo was quite right to shave you. Let me see now . . .

Ernesto despaired at the words *young men*: they cut

him to the quick. When he was thirteen or fourteen he
had longed to be — and be thought — a grown man,
and had pestered his mother to buy him a waistcoat
(like the one the boy had who sat next to him at
school), but nowadays he was glad when he read
articles in the newspaper which referred to someone
his age as 'a boy'. If his mother had said *boys* instead of
*young men* he would have forgiven the missing kiss.

It was underhand, he said, he never asked if I
wanted it or not — he tricked me.

Now go and change your jacket, his mother was
saying, and come straight in for lunch. I've made
*fugazette* for you, and your aunt and I are both hungry.
We've been waiting more than half an hour.

His mother's *fugazette* were his favourite food
(always excepting cakes). Made of minced beef which
Signora Celestina spiced with garlic, they were soaked
in oil for a day and a night, then fried in the same oil
mixed with a little blood. They were, in a word, a sort
of meatball but flat, and with a secret ingredient, and
after his mother's death Ernesto never found their
flavour again, despite the fact that Signora Celestina
entrusted the recipe to her daughter-in-law during a
rare truce, not long before she died.

Until he was thirteen Ernesto would be given one;
then two, just as big as before. Normally he could eat
three or even four, but today he was not hungry for
any sort of food. He ate in silence, withdrew to his
room — the only one in the house with a sloping roof —
as soon as he could, and threw himself on the brass bed
to brood on his gloom. The blackbird was used to
being released at this time of day for its bath, and it
hopped from perch to perch now, calling to its friend
to open the cage.

Ernesto's pondering and gloom all led to one con-
clusion: *If only I could lose my virginity today — now — at
once!* His self-made promise not to go with women
before he was eighteen or nineteen was forgotten.
With a sort of regret he remembered how many of his
schoolmates had already done it, and bragged when
they told him about it. They became experts overnight, and the lessons they gave were richly detailed
. . . Even that cousin of his, who was only the same
age as him (not exactly: he was three months older than
Ernesto) had done it — and more than once, if he was
to be believed.

*If he has, why shouldn't I?* What he had done with the
man did not count: in this sense, life began the day a
boy had a woman for the first time. There were diseases, of course (his mates used to talk about those as
well; one of them even boasted about catching a dose)
but they did not scare him, not just then — not the ones
you catch from women, at any rate. Once, it was true,
he had been obsessed by the idea that he was doomed
to die of consumption before he was twenty; it was the
result of a 'press campaign' against THE MERCILESS
SCOURGE, which terrified readers, especially the
younger ones, and recommended precautions and
cures which in the society of the time were only available to the rich. Everybody else (and Ernesto counted
himself among them) could go to hell. The obsession
lasted two or three months, until the violin appeared
on the scene: the anxieties it brought also cured him.
Then came the relationship with the man.

The difficulty lay elsewhere. He knew he was incapable of saying no, most of all to a woman. So if he
went to a brothel, he would have to accept the first
woman he was offered, and what if he didn't like her?
— if he preferred one of the others? How could he
slight the poor woman with a humiliating refusal?

(*The Worker* had taught him that all prostitutes are unfortunates — victims of bourgeois social prejudice.) Ernesto had not reached the aesthetic age (he would do soon, but travelling by other routes and other means); his sympathies were ruled solely by the sensuality of the moment, and his was a very fickle sensuality, unsure — clearly enough — even of its desires. For instance, he had never wondered if the man was handsome or not; he responded to him for reasons which had nothing aesthetic about them: he wanted to be loved, and the man loved him. (Of course there were other, deeper reasons, but the boy was not conscious of them.) Now a prostitute could not love him, and he knew it: she would go with him for money and would rather have an old man, Signor Wilder or someone like that, who might give her something extra. This matter of choosing (or rather, of not-choosing) was a real difficulty for him, one which was rooted in his character.

But this time again fate smiled. There was a woman in the heart of the old city who worked at her profession alone (perhaps secretly, without a licence from the police). Ernesto had often seen her at the window; once he even thought she smiled at him. She lived on the first floor in an old building in the quarter where all the brothels were. A friend had even told him her rate (a florin); but Ernesto did not know which was her door. If he knocked at the wrong one what could he say to whoever opened it? He pictured — who can say why? — an old woman chasing him down the street with her broom as soon as she realized what he was after, screaming abuse and disgracing him in front of everybody. What was more, the shops owned by his guardian uncle (who, fearing solitary vices, gave his nephew the weekly present for just this purpose, but alas! without ever spelling it out) were in a side street not far from the brothels. What if he passed by that very moment and saw everything? He was quite capable of slapping his face in public, dragging him home by his wrist to stop him wriggling free, and telling his mother the whole story, and Ernesto was sure she would burst into tears — perhaps faint — even expire on the spot in her shame at having such a son. Caught between going and staying, by the need to know what it was that Bernardo had unintentionally set in motion with that untimely, too-early shave, Ernesto resolved to throw everything to chance: he would go to the street where the woman lived and walk past three times; if she appeared at the window he would signal to her and go up; if not, he would come home. The afternoon was virtually his own: he did not need to go to the office till late, just round the city on various business (there were no carts to load or unload that day) before calling by in the evening to present the bills and accounts to scrupulous Signor Wilder. So there was plenty of time. He knew people only went to prostitutes furtively, at night, but he didn't want to wait: he wanted to face everything *now*, in broad daylight (it was a cloudless day, too). If he had stopped to think, what courage he still had would have drained away.

The woman was at her window and she saw him straightaway. Ernesto's heart was in his mouth as he climbed the stairs and found her waiting in the doorway. She looked a little older close to than from the street, but this was a minor detail and did not matter much; more, he instinctively realized it was probably better for him this way. What he did rather notice was the down on her upper lip. What if it grows into a moustache? he wondered. This was an amusing notion and it cheered him up.

As soon as he entered he noticed the odour in her

little room. It was fresh linen, newly sewn — the same odour he used to like so much in his nanny's house. His nanny's husband was an invalid and she had to earn a living for them both; she spent her afternoons at her sewing machine, making bed linen which she sold — or did her best to sell — in the Piazza Ponterosso every morning. But she did not have a licence (nor, perhaps, did this woman), so she had to make her sales as she walked about. (Ernesto often wanted to stop on his way home from the Dante Alighieri School to say hello to his 'second mother' and tell her about his academic triumphs, but she was afraid of the police and always shooed him away. In Franz Josef's day no one could stop her walking here and there with linen under her arm, but if she found a customer they had to catch one another's eye and vanish under a doorway, where the purchaser used the poor woman's illegality to get the stuff cheaply.) This woman made bed linen too, but she did it for herself and her clients — she was very careful about hygiene. Maybe she was an ordinary good woman with repressed maternal instincts; if so, this strange client who had turned up in the middle of the day — and soon proved to be even younger than his years — might have been expressly sent to draw them out. Another thing Ernesto noticed, reminding him again of his nanny's house, was a little lamp burning beneath an image of the Madonna, not far from the double bed with its freshly laundered sheets.

I bet you haven't flown the nest yet, have you, said the woman, feeling Ernesto's embarrassment, for he was neither taking off his own clothes nor laying a hand on hers.

Ernesto both understood and did not understand her.

I've never been with a woman before, he confessed.
Oh you poor love! the woman thought out loud.

She looked at Ernesto more closely. He was a handsome boy — and how different to her usual night-time
visitors! She did not understand but she sensed something: sensed that fate had sent her this afternoon a
strange, unaccountable gift.

Don't be scared, she said, leave it to me. Take your
clothes off now.

The woman began to undress. Ernesto copied her.

Shall I take my stockings off too? she asked meekly.
Ernesto shrugged, as if to say it made no difference to
him. The woman kept them on.

He was so hesitant, she wondered for a moment if it
was not a case of first-time impotence. But a glance
told her that she was wrong, and she was glad. Ernesto
got up when he had finished undressing; he stood
naked before her, arms hanging down, as she sat on the
bed.

Why don't you come and lie down by me? she said,
and he was moving to do so when she changed her
mind and motioned him to stop:

No, we'll do it another way, it'll be easier for you if
it's true this is your first time.

Something in his face assured her that he had not
lied. For that matter why should he lie? Young men
want people to think they are old hands, not raw
recruits, and the more they show off as the former the
more likely they are to be the latter. But Ernesto was
different; his strength and weakness both lay in
showing himself so far as possible as he truly was.
There was nothing calculated in this; it was simply a
way of being, of self-defence too, which is just as valid
as the other way — perhaps more so — but which is
worthless if it is an act. Like all boys his age Ernesto
loved praise, but with the difference in his case that he
had to feel it was deserved. Sometimes he was an-
guished by his relationship with the man: if everyone

who abhorred what they did together and made it a
term of abuse, knew about their relationship, most of
the people who were fond of him now wouldn't be so
any longer. So he thought he had their affection 'on
false pretences', and his young sensibility often suffered as a result.

Meanwhile, to arouse him, the woman had begun to
caress him. Naked, he seemed scarcely more than a
little boy, and she stroked his buttocks as if that were
all he was. They were so soft and smooth, she could
not help her hand lingering there. Ernesto was reminded of the man, and the memory of him in this
place was threatening. What can *she* want with my
arse? he wondered.

You're a poppet, and very handsome too, the
woman said, but still a bit young. Never mind, I like
you better as you are. What's your name?

Prostitutes usually never ask men this question, and
if they give a name themselves it is never their true one.
But Ernesto was not an ordinary client.

Ernesto, he replied, giving his surname too.

The woman smiled.

Mine's Tanda, she said. When I lived at home (she
did not say where this was) and was like all the other
women, it was Natascia.

So she was a Slovene from the Territory. It was
something else she had in common with Ernesto's
nanny; perhaps these coincidences were making everything more awkward.

Come, the woman said as she lay back on the bed,
this is the best way for you — and she drew the boy to
her.

Ernesto's pleasure was great but it was not new to
him. Surely he had experienced it before, known it
more than once — known it always, even before he
was born. He felt like a man arriving home after a

perilous voyage, returning to the place where he knows everything and now finds it again: how the furniture is arranged, where the cupboards are — everything. When he rose from the bed, heartened, the woman filled a bowl with water, added some liquid which stained it light pink, and washed Ernesto's abashed member. It was a ritual, a *post facto* precaution against disease, which clients liked and demanded. Ernesto was no longer afraid on his own account, and he asked why she did this.

It's for hygiene, the woman explained. I haven't any diseases and would have told you if I had, or I'd have given you a condom anyway. But it's what men want, and if I'm to make a living I have to keep them all happy. I'd feel like a murderer if you caught anything from me.

I'm not frightened of diseases, said Ernesto, and as he wanted to be on his way (to think in peace over all that had happened), he dug into his pocket for some money to pay her. It was the first of the month and the first day of the week, so he was rich. He gave her almost all he had (she only charged a florin), including what he had forgotten to pay Bernardo.

It's too much, she protested, amazed at the boy's generosity. (Only old or impotent men paid so well, and the pleasure he had brought her — not so much physical — was payment more than enough.) She could not persuade Ernesto to take back some of his money.

If you ever want to come back, she said when Ernesto was at the door, do, and never mind if you don't have any money. Don't forget my name — Tanda — and don't forget which door: there's a bad woman in the room next door, I don't want you to end up with her. Remember, a lad like you doesn't have to pay every time. You'll always be welcome, with money or without. — She was touched, and wished she could kiss him. But she saw his impatience to be off (she knew that impatience of men) and did not dare.

Two things aggravated Ernesto as he went on his way to make the calls for Signor Wilder: he could not free the tangled skein of his thoughts, and he was very thirsty. The snags would not begin to be loosened for many years, but he could quench his thirst (there are physiological reasons why men are always thirsty after intercourse with a prostitute) straightaway. But he wanted to quench it with a raspberry crush and had given so much money to the woman that, reckoning up, there was not enough left for a visit to a sweetshop even if he ignored the cakes and restricted himself to a single drink — which to make matters worse he could picture already, ice-cold and glistening. So he had no choice but a public water-fountain, and he found one away from the centre, in a densely populated suburb of Trieste. The city was spreading in all directions: old, shabby houses which Ernesto remembered from his childhood walks and had always assumed would stand forever, were being knocked down for new building. A factory chimney poured out thick smoke, blackening the surrounding air, and workers were already streaming out of the factories, their food boxes under their arms. *All comrades, all socialists*, thought Ernesto, wanting to be one of them. But the sight sharply reminded him that he was late, and suddenly, unusually, he felt nostalgic for the office, even nostalgic for Signor Wilder. There was no work for the man today, so he wouldn't be there. He decided to spend his last few coppers on a tram ticket to speed him on his way; the fare could always be charged to tight-fisted Signor Wilder.

The water fountain stood in the middle of a tree-lined piazza between a barracks and a church, both painted yellow ochre. There was a crowd of women waiting their turn, young for the most part and some mere children, all carrying pitchers, washbasins and other vessels on their heads; for in those days very few houses had piped water, which was considered a great luxury. Although his thirst was parching, Ernesto was ready to wait patiently in the queue, and Lord knows how long he would have been standing there if an old, white-haired woman had not called out to the others, Hey! Let this poor lamb have his drink! Don't you see he's dying of thirst?

Poor lamb — poor love: almost the prostitute's very words. This latest coincidence made him uncomfortable. The women moved aside for Ernesto, who thanked the old crone and went up to the fountain. He had to bend nearly double to reach the spout, and the crouching posture of his body stirred an unwelcome memory. Just then he heard laughter at his back.

They know everything, he thought. They know about the man and they know where I've been today: somehow they can see it written all over me, that's why they're laughing. — Though his thirst was not yet quenched he stopped drinking and went away scarlet-faced. Lost in his dismay, he did not notice that the women who were laughing (and laughing not at but with him) were nearly all very young; in some cases very pretty too. They gazed at Ernesto, but he kept his eyes on the ground and tried to escape from the wretched fountain as fast as he could.

He judged himself too harshly; there was nothing to laugh at in his appearance — nothing in the least effeminate. The young women were laughing because they were about the same age as Ernesto and knew no other way to attract his eye. Perhaps there was not one of them who would not have been delighted by a compliment — not have hoarded the least show of interest in her heart for a few hours or days. But Ernesto interpreted their soft laughter differently. So the day which had started with Bernardo's treacherous shave now ended badly. Ages seemed to have passed since he had had a woman for the first time . . . A whole epoch separated him from the beginning of that strange friendship with a labourer who — he was sure of this, at least — had loved him in his way, and perhaps (had Ernesto so wished) would love him still . . . And only a month had gone by.

## Fourth Episode

There was an innovation in the office when Ernesto went to work next day. Another, younger boy was sitting at the far side of the desk, his back to the window. Ernesto saw what was happening at once; this, he said to himself, is competition.

In those days commercial apprentices were much in demand in the Piazza at Trieste, and probably in piazzas the small world over; for whether they worked well or poorly they cost nothing in return. There were advertisements every day in the classified columns of the *Piccolo* and the other local papers (except *The Worker*) under the heading EMPLOYMENT OFFERED AND SOUGHT, and worded thus: 'Unpaid apprentice, calligraphy first-class, seeks useful position in . . .'

Or: 'German essential. Apply for details . . .' et cetera.

An apprenticeship lasted between six months and a year, during which period the boy earned nothing at all. If he was not sacked beforehand or had not resigned with something better under his belt, he then 'joined the payroll' at ten crowns a month. The new boy facing Ernesto over his own desktop must have been the result of one such classified advertisement; Signor Wilder must have chosen him from a band of contenders the previous afternoon, or some other time when Ernesto was away from the office.

While he was not fond of his employer, Ernesto did not — for all his naughty tricks and caricatures — loathe him, and he was certainly loyal wherever work was concerned. Signor Wilder was a family figure, rather comic and not particularly interesting but nothing worse than that. You may remember that Ernesto had been surprised by a sort of nostalgia for the man, almost a desire to see him, as he bent down to drink from the unlucky water fountain. All in all, for Ernesto the boss was a kind of object: the kind which is always to hand, the sight of which can sometimes be comforting: can even dissolve a bad mood. For his part Signor Wilder had never shown any special dislike of Ernesto — had even, however (un)suitably, regaled him with a silver-headed cane; and his monthly salary (which Ernesto certainly believed was well earned for the wear on his legs alone) was a little higher than it might have been, given the average rates of pay on one hand and his employer's meanness on the other. So it was all the more of a blow now to find himself up against a rival. He felt betrayed: an 'innocent' victim of the thing he feared most of all (Ernesto was a dog, not a cat). But still, he should make quite sure about the newcomer before blaming Signor Wilder.

Who are you? he asked.

The other boy stood up before replying.

So I'm the head clerk, thought Ernesto, who secretly cherished two somewhat conflicting ambitions neither of which would be fulfilled by life. Although he did not like his work — quite the opposite — he still aspired (the human heart is as mysterious as this!) to be head clerk of an important firm in the city, preferably one dealing with colonial trade (this last detail can probably be traced to his stamp-collecting days); and at the same time yearned to be a famous violinist. He would have preferred the second of these, needless to say: what with the travelling, the applause and adoration of the audience, a concert artist's life looked like heaven on earth. But deep in his heart he did not really believe it was possible. He was not weak in the head, after all; quite apart from the relatively late age at which he had started taking lessons, he knew it would never be easy for someone who still could not tune his own instrument after two years (one chord or another always dropped or rose a little in pitch) to follow in the footsteps of that great Bohemian, whose perfect tone was admired by all the critics.

I'm the new apprentice, answered the standing boy. Signor Wilder engaged me yesterday and told me to come this morning. And he said to sit on this chair here at this desk.

Ernesto was nonplussed. The longer he looked at the boy the worse he seemed. He had dull blond hair, a triangular face, and grey eyes that flitted here and there like mice in a cage. And even at this distance he smelled like a wild animal. If Ernesto had been a more experienced physiognomist he would have seen straightaway that he was dealing with one of those people who are destined to 'succeed in life'; destined, that is, to become head clerks at the age of forty — not only in their dreams but in reality, and what's more, to their immense satisfaction.

He ordered the boy to sit down; then he introduced himself. The boy's name was Stefano, and his surname revealed Slavic origins.

What a boy! thought Ernesto, though not because of his race, for he was a good, loyal Italian but no fanatic; today he would be called a patriot but not a nationalist. Besides, he was a socialist and, probably thanks to the influence of his 'second mother', he harboured no loathing for the Slavs, unlike other Triestines of his class (such as his cousin). He took against the boy for other reasons.

The recruit sat down again and answered all Ernesto's questions, but lukewarmly, without ever

looking at his interlocutor for more than half a second.
Then he tried to appear coolly at ease (for likeable or
not, he was still a boy — and in his first day at work,
what's more) by organizing the part of the desk
assigned to him: pen and pencils on one side, inkstand
in the middle, writing paper in a pile on the other side,
graded by size. (Perhaps too he was disconcerted by
the sheer amount of stationery.) Plainly he was embarrassed, as his eyes and even these gestures showed,
and he did not know how to behave with Ernesto. Was
he really his superior? Could he be a relative of Signor
Wilder? Or a protégé? Native caution advised the most
respectful attitude — it could not do any harm, whatever the truth — towards this boy who was roughly his
own age and with whom it would have been more than
natural to use *tu* straightaway and start grousing about
the boss. Nor could Ernesto think what to say after he
had asked about his school and his German, or lack of
it. Then, when there could be no doubt that Signor
Wilder himself had indeed told Stefano to sit here (so
that he, Ernesto, would be face to face with him all
day), he had a flash of inspiration: he would teach him
how to keep the letter-book up to date — the first skill
apprentices had to learn, he knew. Signor Wilder,
usually so punctual, was keeping them waiting this
morning. The first thing he did when he finally arrived
was call Ernesto into his study.

I've engaged a new apprentice, he began. *Sie werden
sehen* — and he continued in German almost for the rest
of the meeting. — You'll see how fast and well he
catches on. First of all teach him to be tidy. — This was
a tacit rebuke for what he thought was Ernesto's own
untidiness. Signor Wilder seemed to have quite forgotten the basic sympathy he had always implied for
the *verfluchte Kerl*. But perhaps his suspicions were
belatedly roused over the extravagant use of naph-

thalene for cleaning — those inexplicable smudges on
his five-page letters — the urchins who burst through
Ernesto's door and chased each other screaming out of
his own — the self-destructing gas-lamps — the
canary-coloured gloves, etc. etc; and he had found a
way to avenge himself on the guilty party without
actually sacking him. He was useful for the Italian
correspondence, after all, and distrustful as he was by
nature or frailty, he had never doubted Ernesto's
honesty. He divided the work between the two boys in
such a way that once the apprentice had been trained
there would, at least in theory, be precious little left for
Ernesto to do . . . Effectively he would have the Italian
correspondence, collecting the bills, and supervising
the labourers — and he would happily pass on the last
of these to the newcomer, because of the man . . . Not
exactly head clerk after all! he thought. It's the sack
sure enough, except Signor Wilder wants me to sack
myself, though God knows why.

If the reader does not already agree that Ernesto was
an idiot, he soon will. But he had his good qualities
too; for example, he found it difficult to tell lies, and
even at this age he could not accept any favour (even, in
this case, Signor Wilder's wage) unless he felt he could
repay it in full. Otherwise he was simply irritated and
uneasy. (Need we add that the second quality was even
more harmful to him in everyday life?) So his impulse
was to resign on the spot and let Signor Wilder have
the bother of training his new apprentice. But he
thought of his mother: of the tears and scenes that
would follow his self-dismissal. It also crossed his
mind that he might be misjudging Signor Wilder's real
intentions: what if he was simply expanding his
business and needed a new employee for the extra
work? If that was the case he was not being punished at
all, for whatever work the boss took away with one

hand would be restored with the other — he might even give back too much. In the last years of the nineteenth century, business involved risks which do not obtain today, in 1953; bankruptcies were the order of the day, so to speak, often ending with a pistol shot in the bankrupt's mouth or temple (rarely in the heart), whether he was crooked or not. In business, as in everything else, Signor Wilder was very prudent; obsessed by the idea of failure (not that Ernesto could have known this) he had even gone so far as to buy a revolver in case his worst fears ever came true. They never did, and Signor Wilder — who was not really an old man, whatever the sixteen-year-old Ernesto might think — would yet participate in the First World War as a Reserve Officer (non-combattant), then leave Trieste after the Italian occupation (which he took as a personal affront) and live on well into the Second War, in conditions which need no describing; and would die in a gas oven with a batch of other Hungarian Jews who were sought out and annihilated by the Germany he loved so much, which saw him — he was over eighty at the time and already senile — as a dangerous enemy of the thousand-year Reich . . . This was the fate of the person sitting before Ernesto now, sharing the peaceful little jobs between the two boys; and not his fate alone . . . There was no mention of dismissals or pay reductions, and he closed his little address with a few words in Italian which were almost affectionate (but they seemed critical to Ernesto all the same). For a moment he was even tempted to confide his plans for the expansion that he was indeed considering; but at the last moment it seemed wiser not to tell a soul, not yet, not even the *verfluchte Kerl* — the bloody boy.

Not long afterwards, Ernesto was sitting on top of a cartload of flour sacks next to the man, on the way back from the port, where he had been settling some business at the customs house for Signor Wilder. He had almost forgotten the new apprentice, whom he found he could keep in his place easily enough; he had even managed to turn him into a sort of personal valet: whenever he had a bit of money to spare and the temptation was too much, he sent him — be it morning, afternoon, or whenever — to a nearby baker, one of Signor Wilder's customers whose cakes made up in size what they lacked in quality, to buy four tarts — the same ones the man used to bring for him. He tried to share them (be it said to his credit) half and half with Stefano, who always fended him off with effusive thanks and hollow refusals which never failed to irritate Ernesto. He talked to him in dialect now, not Italian, and used *tu*, while finding it quite in order for the apprentice, who was only a year younger, to keep using *lei* like a subordinate. He would have found *tu* equally acceptable, but as he didn't like him (although their relations were perfectly cordial) he deliberately never mentioned the matter.

The man was sulky, acting as if the boy was not there. Yet Ernesto felt unusually cheerful and light-hearted this morning. He gazed admiringly at the people walking busily along, crowding the streets of Trieste. The women carried shopping bags or baskets on their arms, and everyone seemed to have something very important to do. Looking up and down the streets as they rode, he saw now a strip of sea, now the hills, both appearing much closer in the marvellous summery light than they really were. What a beautiful city Trieste is, thought Ernesto for the first time in his life, I did well to be born here (as if he had had any choice). Then it struck him that it was the only city he

had ever seen, and he remembered how he used to
envy a luckier classmate at school who spent long
periods of the holidays travelling abroad with his
parents, and told wonderful tales on his return. He had
no means of comparison, so he could not know how
accurate his judgement was. Every judgement implies
comparison, and the very impossibility of comparing
made Ernesto less sure that he was right — as in fact he
was.

The man was sulking because Ernesto had not said a
word to him except in the course of work since the day
he broke up the birch wand chosen with such loving
care to give him a 'little punishment' (but more truly to
release the sadistic element which seems inseparable
from this kind of love). Ernesto always picked him
when he came to the Piazza for a labourer, but that was
all. Kids are all the same, thought the man, they get
bored after a few times and always leave you if you
don't leave them first. But the wound lay deeper than
this, for he knew too well that Ernesto was and would
remain unique in his dismal existence; that once lost he
could never hope to replace him, not with all the 'kids'
in the world. The bitterness of his love sometimes
sharpened into a bitterness at society: Ernesto treats me
like this because he's one of the gentry and I'm a
pauper, he would think at such moments. But he was
mistaken; beside the fact that the boy thought of himself as a poor person too, he was hardly aware of the
social differences; and perhaps he wouldn't have done
with a 'gentleman' what he had done with a labourer.

Trieste is beautiful — Ernesto said it aloud this time
— and Diem (the boy he used to sit next to at school,
the one who had prompted his yearning for a waistcoat) can boast about those other cities to his heart's
content, none of them can be as lovely as this . . . But
as he was boasting about his own city he noticed that

he was hunching his shoulders and leaning forward (his mother often scolded him for this habit). I've grown too fast, he thought mournfully, for in his eyes being a little taller than the average was a defect, one cause of his self-declared 'ugliness'. He sat up straight, lamenting that he was not just half-a-head shorter. Then his hazel eyes settled on the man, who had his red kerchief tied round his head as usual. At first it gave him a certain satisfaction to see him so dejected (he easily guessed the reason, though never suspected the social grudge he bore); he was pleased with an inner delight at his own 'power' over someone so much older than himself, and pleased at the same time by this proof that after all he was not too 'ugly' for anyone to love him; then he felt a pang, almost of guilt. In short, he wanted to laugh.

You look like Ali Baba, he told the man, who glared at him.

I'm no 'baba' and you should know it by now, he retaliated, mistaking the proper name for a noun which was insulting to a man in his state.

Ernesto laughed louder, almost as loudly as he had laughed that first day about the cocoa butter cones. Then he explained that Ali Baba was the character in the fairy tale that came, like the Three Kings, from the Orient, and it had nothing to do with girls.

He did the same job as you, he added, and wore something red on his head as well.

The reader needs to know that Ernesto had spent the most enchanting summer of his life when he was thirteen and pining for the waistcoat, reading *The Arabian Nights* as he lay on his tummy on the brass bed in the only room in the house with a sloping roof. He was so engrossed that he even forgot to go swimming in the sea, which he normally looked forward to so much. That same happy summer his nanny's husband

gave him Pimpo the blackbird, and the wonder he felt
as he watched the bird's behaviour and habits merged
blissfully and unforgettably with the wonder stirred in
him by the book of tales. He was especially delighted
by the story of a boy — he couldn't remember his
name — who finds the father he had never known:
finds him as he is wandering through the alleys of a
foreign city with his slave at his side. After many
adventures the father was now a confectioner in this
same city (Baghdad — or was it Basra?) and did not
even recognize his son, whom he had last seen as a tiny
baby. But blood called to blood, or perhaps he was
drawn to the youth's extraordinary beauty, for he
invited him to try a sherbet ice, free of charge,
swearing they were incomparably the best in the city.
The boy was under the strictest orders never to eat
away from home or talk to anyone whosoever, and the
slave wouldn't have accepted the invitation at any
price. But the confectioner and the boy were so
pressing, they eventually overcame his terror of the
punishment which was bound to follow, should their
offence ever be discovered. The sherbet ice was so
delicious the boy was easily persuaded to have another.
Then he wanted to return every day, despite the slave's
pleas (he had yielded once, so was now in his master's
power), or rather he wanted their walks to have this
purpose and no other. Needless to say, they were
found out (the youth ate so many ices one afternoon
that he had no room for supper and had to confess
everything to his mother); the slave was flogged till he
bled, and the boy's parents — still deeply in love —
found each other again and were reunited, thanks to
the sherbet ices. Ernesto had been especially impressed
by the boy's exclamation when the confectioner, ever
more fascinated by his guest's beauty, wanted to pass
from words to caresses. The boy (who would have

been about Ernesto's age that summer) stepped back, with this command: *Stay where you are. Be content to watch and serve me.* (Ernesto would have given anything in the world to be that boy, if only for five minutes.) That evening Signora Celestina was anxious and vexed to see him still so absorbed in his book; she gave him a few coins to go out for a breath of air and buy himself a little ice cream. He went to the Caffè del Tergesteo, which used to put tables outside at the height of summer facing the Teatro Communale (now the Teatro Verdi). It was a rather genteel café, popular with rich businessmen, nearly all of them old men and some from faraway Turkey, wearing red fez hats like the people in *The Arabian Nights*. No one paid any attention to Ernesto (oh how lucky that other boy had been!) except the waiter, who overlooked his tender years and off-the-peg clothes and treated him like a grown-up, a proper gentleman, bringing out the 'little ice cream' he had chosen with great care and hesitation from the silver-framed list the waiter had presented with a flourish. (But it never crossed the waiter's mind to offer him free of charge a second 'little ice cream' . . .) With its merchants, red fez hats, and such ice cream as, were he still alive, Ernesto would not find anywhere today, the café only encouraged his fantasies, and with his inner eye he went on reading *The Arabian Nights* (which he possessed, of course, in the thoroughly bowdlerised version by the Frenchman Galland, put into Italian by that upright and public-spirited publisher, Adriano Salani). So, that memorable summer the boy not only discovered the Orient which has been called *a beggar's dream* and is given voice in Scheherazade's stories (Napoleon defined the other, more real Orient when he said, and as usual said truly, *The Orient is a cur*), but also the elegance of the French eighteenth century. Yet he was not conscious of either discovery, did not even know how happy he was. When he became aware of these things many years later — as he did: very clearly aware — everything in and around him was so changed that memories which should have consoled him were made painful by their contrast with present anguish.

The man's interest in fairy tales (Oriental or otherwise) was very limited, and it was in vain that Ernesto told him the story of *Open sesame!* with Ali Baba as the hero. Still, he was glad the boy was talking to him, whatever the subject: it was like old times returning.

Have you forgotten already what we used to do together and liked so much? he asked, a final trace of bitterness in his voice.

You told me people wind up in prison for doing these things, Ernesto replied with real or sham solemnity.

This time the argument seemed to have no effect on the man.

God punishes, Ernesto added, for once thoroughly hypocritical, as he had lost faith the day he masturbated for the first time, after his corrupting cousin's ever-shining example. He would have better achieved his goal of liberation from the man by telling him he had already been with a woman and was looking for ways to save money for another visit to Tanda (he wanted to savour more consciously the pleasure he had tasted rather feverishly the first time). The man did not dislike women, but he never slept with them, and if he had known that Ernesto had been with a woman he might no longer have desired him anyway.

If you like, continued the man, I'll tell him I tore one of the sacks and have to mend it. That can be our excuse, so we can be in the usual place . . .

You've lost your head, Ernesto said irritably. Next you'll want to be doing it with the door open . . .

There's only the carter and he needs to keep his eye on the horses. I'm only asking to touch you . . . I'll come in a moment, I promise . . .

He spoke not only *sottovoce* but like a down-and-out, a true down-and-out begging for alms, and Ernesto (who did not want to torment the man and was even a bit scared of him) was touched.

All right, he said, if not now, then after lunch. But it's the last time.


Ernesto kept his word, as he usually did, and the man, who removed his kerchief for the occasion, so revealing a head of black gypsy hair, even managed to brush his cheek with a kiss. But now the boy knew there was only one way to be free of the man: he must resign, or better still make Signor Wilder dismiss him.

Rather than stay in the office Ernesto had always preferred the tasks which involved going out to the port or into the suburbs, and with the new apprentice installed at his desk he preferred them more than ever. Although he was healthy he was not a robust boy — despite the best efforts of *Ischirogeno*, the fashionable new patent tonic medicine with which the old doctor and Signora Celestina tried to replace the hated cod-liver oil — and it wore him out to be on his feet all day, especially now summer had arrived. I'm ready to drop by the evening, he said to the man one day, complaining about the night classes which, the reader may recall, he had to attend when all he wanted to do was go straight to bed and sleep. Now the classes had finished for the term, but Ernesto still felt 'dead tired' — as he said to his mother, laying it on thickly — when he came home from work. Signor Wilder put a small sum of money at his disposal to cover his 'overheads', including tram tickets. Ernesto knew how parsi-

monious his employer was and anyway he did not
abuse this privilege, often going by foot even when he
was tired. He didn't like the trams now they were no
longer horse-drawn. A carriage would have been
better — yes, that would have suited him very well.
Sometimes he forgot he was a socialist and had visions
of a twin-horse carriage with a liveried groom at the
reins. His old aunt — the one with the money — sat
behind with Ernesto, who was making business calls
in this stately fashion for Signor Wilder. . . They were
both elegantly dressed, the aunt as befitted a lady of a
certain age, and he as an adored son . . . But recently,
he had been making do more and more with the trams
(a few were still horse-drawn, the last of their kind),
particularly when he had to travel as far out as Roiano,
where the tree-lined piazza with the water fountain
was, and where Signor Wilder had several customers
among the bakers and confectioners, some of them in
arrears. Every Friday Ernesto submitted an account of
his expenses and Signor Wilder reimbursed him without, it must be said, asking questions. But on the
Friday of the week in which Ernesto resolved to free
himself of the man, his employer passed an unusual
and ill-timed remark about these to-his-mind-too-
frequent 'trips' by tram; and he said it in a coarse
manner. It was fate announcing itself for the second
time, and again via Signor Wilder, whose 'mission' it
would appear to have been first to enable his apprentice's relationship with the man, then to help him break
it off. Ernesto said nothing at the time, but the
moment he was back in his little room he took a sheet
of headed paper and without exactly tendering his
resignation, swiftly wrote an insulting letter to Signor
Wilder.

Although we know so much about Ernesto — too
much, perhaps — we have unfortunately forgotten the

precise wording of his letter, which has since been lost, like so much else in the world. (What a pity! Who knows if some collector of curios and autographs might not now — in August 1953 — pay a fair price for it?) We only know that it began *Dear Signor Wilder*, that the *dear Signor* was then accused of exploiting the undersigner's long legs; that he was even called a *skin-flint* (the word was both underlined and crossed out, but not so carefully that a determined reader could not decipher it through the scorings — and Signor Wilder was a determined reader, surely enough); and that it closed with a frigid *Cordial regards*, in the style of the business correspondence Ernesto conducted on his employer's behalf. The new apprentice had overheard the boss criticizing Signor Ernesto's extravagance on the tramways, and now he craned his neck to read whatever his 'immediate superior' was writing with brow so furrowed. He could only make out the name of the addressee, but it was not hard to guess the rest, and it slowly dawned even on Stefano (a boy wholly devoid of imagination) that what Ernesto was writing so fluently that he seemed inspired, was either his formal notice of resignation or a letter which could very well lead to the sack. Ernesto finished and signed the letter, and asked Stefano for an envelope (it so happened envelopes were kept in his part of the desk) which he superscribed with his employer's full name in capital letters. Then he tiptoed into his study and laid it on his desk in full view, taking advantage of a moment when the addressee was searching for something in his half-opened safe. If he made any sound Signor Wilder (who only ever opened the safe when quite alone and with the utmost circumspection, although it held nothing but account books: both his own — which were correct — and the ones for the tax inspector, which were slightly less so) would certainly round on

the intruder . . . A few minutes later, when Signor
Wilder had opened Ernesto's provocative letter (i.e.
swallowed the bait) the apprentices old and new both
heard, with different emotions, half-choked mutter-
ings and colourful abuse, including a *verfluchte Kerl*,
emerge from the old man's study. For his own sake the
bloody boy should not have stayed in the vicinity.
Eventually a rather squat, red-faced man, looking
more like Ernesto's caricature than usual, appeared in
the doorway connecting the two rooms. It was a very
hot day too, a day to spend by the seaside or in some
shady place in the country, not shut up in an office, and
tempers were frayed in that climate which breeds
revolutions.

Crazy, mannerless boy, Signor Wilder began
loudly, with no preamble, then proceeded half in
Italian (*his* Italian) and half in German to upbraid
Ernesto for his behaviour not only today but always,
*culimating* (he meant culminating) in this *insolent* letter.
Was this the language to use with his employer? With
someone who had been so good to him and, for his
lady mother's sake, so *geduld* (patient), even (he now
saw) to *excess*? And he flapped the letter under
Ernesto's nose as he moaned. If he was sick and could
not walk properly at his age, he should get himself
cured while there was still time. (Just wait, thought
Ernesto, almost enjoying this, he'll be prescribing
*Ischirogeno* too, if not cod-liver oil.) His office was not a
*Krankenhaus* (hospital), nor an institution for the cor-
rection of vicious, ignorant rascals. Look at your colleague here, Herr Stefano, he added, and follow his
example. (If Ernesto was entertained by Signor
Wilder's wrath, he glowered now to hear the
triangular-faced apprentice not only named but held
up as a model. The paragon himself, meanwhile,
lowered his grey eyes, to relish the praise from so

powerful a person as Signor Wilder seemed to him then more than ever, without revealing his vast satisfaction; lowered them just at the right moment to the letter-book, for he was updating the index, which Ernesto had badly neglected.) Signor Wilder pressed ruthlessly on: Look at this splendid boy, so much younger than you (he was one year younger) yet he not only writes a much better hand (a serious charge against a copy clerk — what the labourer called a *penman* — when the first typewriters in Europe were still cumbersome, luxurious things, not at all widely used), but in the few weeks he has been with me (he had been with Ernesto, not with him) he's also learned more than you know after nearly two years, you arrogant, scatterbrained young man. (Not true: Ernesto wasn't in the least arrogant, and despite his native untidiness he gave back more than Stefano would do after years of trying, for what little Stefano knew he had learned from Ernesto, including how to update the letter-book.) Me, an exploiter of my boys' legs, me a skinflint, me . . . me . . . me — and he broke off, either because his rage was choking him or because he had some reason of his own for not wanting to finish whatever phrase was on his tongue – Right! Consider yourself fired as from now. (He paused again, as if waiting — hoping? — for the newly sacked one to beg forgiveness or at least show some little sign of remorse.) When the culprit made no reply, he continued more ruthlessly than ever: Tomorrow — no, not tomorrow, today, now — send your poor lady mother here to me. She has my deepest sympathy. I shall give her the half-month's pay which I don't owe you, strictly speaking, as you brought this on yourself, and I'll read her the letter, though I'll be very sorry to give so much pain to such a *wohlgeborene Frau* (a well-bred lady). Only a wretched boy like you could have

written such a letter. Leave the petty cash with Stefano
(however grave the matter in hand Signor Wilder
always took care of the details; which did not stop him
losing at Waterloo — yes, him too, as we have already
described, and it was a Waterloo the poor man far from
deserved). Be so good as to collect your things immediately (he meant Ernesto's little books of the
Biblioteca Economica Sonzogna and the pile of papers
he had found in his desk drawers when the boy was ill)
and clear out now — now, do you hear? — out of here
now. They tell me you are learning the violin (he
smiled sneeringly, for which Ernesto — the boy who
did not hate anybody — could happily have strangled
him), but you can't be a good musician, dear sir, unless
you have a good heart (it was a good ear Ernesto
lacked, not a good heart), and that you don't have, oh
no, not a good heart! You don't have one where your
employer is concerned anyway or you could never
have written this letter — And again he brandished it
like a banner in Ernesto's face. He seemed almost in
tears as he denounced this *insolence*, but whether from
indignation or for some other reason was not clear. —
You're an anarchist, that's what you are, and I don't
want anarchists anywhere near me. (He had sometimes seen Ernesto reading *The Worker*, and apart from
the fact that he did not like his staff to read in office
hours even if there was no work to be done, he hated
socialists even more than the uncle did; so he blithely
confused the anarchists with their arch enemies — and
he wasn't the only one . . . But in this case perhaps he
was not far wrong: both as a boy in general and himself
in particular Ernesto was, without knowing it, much
more of an anarchist than a socialist.) So get out, and
don't forget to send your poor lady mother as soon as
she can come . . .

With these last words to someone he would never

see again (unless at a concert, fleetingly, without a word exchanged) he went back into his study, which suddenly looked as bleak as his home across the street. (Married for many years, Signor Wilder had no children.) His tirade had not been as satisfying as he might have hoped; what was more, the *verfluchte Kerl* apparently had no regrets about the letter, or about anything else. It took Ernesto five minutes to gather his things. He handed the petty cash to Stefano with the keys, which meticulous Signor Wilder had somehow forgotten to mention, then left the rooms where he had spent two years of his young life without a word to anyone, not even to the apprentice who automatically took his place. Stefano had a sudden urge to run after him and seize his hand, as one boy with another — there is no one, however barren in spirit, who does not sometimes have a generous impulse. But he remembered Signor Wilder — so much more powerful than the poor sacked boy — and thought of the impression his gesture might make if it were seen; he wasn't brave enough to do that good deed, and he stayed in his place right up to the fatal August of 1914.

I've just been dismissed by Signor Wilder, Ernesto announced in dialect as soon as his mother opened the door. In his eagerness to impart the good news he did not show even a trace of the anguish he had so plainly felt the day Bernardo gave him that treacherous first shave; and she was astonished to see him back at this hour. So she didn't understand; she thought Signor Wilder had given him a day's holiday because there was no work, or something of the sort.

What's that? she asked, still unruffled. (Signora Celestina was indeed a *wohlgeborene Frau*, born of a good family, and even if she did occasionally speak it

herself, she disdained the dialect as something belong-
ing to the 'servant class'.)

I said Signor Wilder just sacked me.

Sacked you! she cried. But why?

Ernesto told her what could be told: the story of the
tram, the money, the letter and so on. His mother
listened in dismay. She did not weep — as Ernesto had
feared she would — nor did she faint. As if worn out,
she slumped into a chair.

Mother — Ernesto wanted to justify himself, but
she cut him short.

What a wretched woman I am, she said, cursed as
wife and mother! First your father, now you. . .

But don't you think I was right? Why should I let
that foul man exploit me? He hasn't raised my pay for
six months, don't forget, and now he even grudges me
the tram fare — in this heat! You should have heard
him! I'll soon find another job just as good, concluded
Ernesto, who would never be employed by anyone
again in all his long life.

And in the mean time? demanded Signora Celestina.
How am I to hide this from your aunt? You know very
well we're dependent on her.

Ernesto made a gesture of exasperation. He could
not remember a time when he had not heard this
argument against himself, against his own existence;
apart from the fact that it was not his fault, he knew his
aunt was rich — even richer than they had led him to
believe in the past for safety's sake. And he knew she
had left all her money to him because his corrupting
cousin had said so; she had already made out her will in
his favour, and the will was safely in a lawyer's strong-
box. Not that Ernesto wanted her to die: he was
genuinely, tenderly fond of her. He remembered how
his mother used to threaten him (with the best of
intentions, of course: what don't mothers do with their

best intentions!) whenever he had not done as well at school as she wanted — that's to say, whenever he brought home a less than first-class report; used to threaten that his aunt would throw them both out of the house, weary of supporting a boy who didn't even know how to be top of the class. He had not believed this vindictive fairy tale (so different to the ones in *The Arabian Nights!*) for years, but it had made him suffer in the past . . . As the date for a school report loomed near, there had been nights when the threat hanging over them made it hard to sleep, as he helplessly followed the train of images stirred in his young brain by his mother's words (seeing them both homeless, wandering the streets of Trieste, vainly begging for pennies . . .). As we say, he no longer took it seriously — but even so . . .

She loves you, he said, she couldn't live without you. Who would take care of her if you weren't here? What would she do at her age (the aunt was well over seventy) by herself? Who would look after her when she's sick? You'll see, when she knows all about it she'll admit I was right. She loves me too, he added, perhaps more than you do, mother. The truth was his aunt adored him, but she was a bit mean and always afraid he would want too much of her money now he was growing up. He already asked for some now and then, only occasionally and for a bit at a time, but she still made him beg before she let him have it. *I'll die in the straw*, she would say, surrendering the little sum he wanted, rarely more than a crown or two, *and it will be your fault*. (She meant: in the most squalid penury, without even a mattress to her name.) Ernesto held back as much as possible because he did not want to be a pest, or for her to think he loved her for her money. Or at least he had held back until now . . . But tonight, for instance, there was a concert he wanted to hear, and he would not have enough for a seat (price: two florins) even if he was willing to use the money set aside (by abjuring cake shops *almost* all the time) for another visit to Tanda. In the past he would have asked Signor Wilder for an advance (the boss used to grumble but never refused him). And he particularly wanted to go to this concert . . .

Signora Celestina was hurt by the comparison between her own and the aunt's affections. She loved her son very much — too much, perhaps — but thought it was her duty not to show it . . . another mistake, but the poor woman did not know. Besides, she thought Ernesto preferred the aunt, because she was rich, to herself, who was poor; and she was jealous. So she began to cry.

Don't, mother, Ernesto said bravely, everything will come right, you'll see. Meanwhile I'll work at my German every day and I'll try to make you happy in every way. Mother — He wanted to say more but felt too close to tears himself. Too much had happened in these last months: more, he thought, than in all the rest of his life; more at any rate than to other boys his age, who were still at school. So he stopped.

Thrown out, and before the end of the month, exclaimed Signora Celestina. What a letter it must have been!

You can read it for yourself, mother, Signor Wilder wants you to go and see him today. At first he said tomorrow, then he changed his mind and said he wishes to see you today and show you the letter. Will you go?

Ernesto was longing for her to go at once, without more ado; in the first place because he hated to see her cry (her tears cut his conscience as nothing else could), then because it would give him a chance, he had just realized, to ask his aunt for some money for the con-

cert. A virtuoso violinist was to perform that night at
the Music Society; Ernesto had heard him the year
before and wanted to hear him again. When he listened
to a great violinist, he identified with him and
imagined the audience's applause ringing round him; it
was this identification he enjoyed most of all, though
he did like music (despite his imperfect ear and Signor
Wilder's sneers), especially chamber music, and this
evening's programme — including J. S. Bach's famous
*Chaconne* for solo violin — was irresistible.

I'll go at once, said Signora Celestina, reassured
somewhat. She supposed it was a question of some
misunderstanding which a few words with Signor
Wilder could easily put right. Mothers can do a lot, she
thought.

Perhaps it's the new boy setting him against you, she
suggested.

No, he doesn't come into it, he said, thinking *If she
only knew why I couldn't wait to get the sack!*

Don't breathe a word of this to your aunt while I'm
gone, warned his mother. If she wants to know why
you're here, say you didn't feel well and asked for the
day off . . . Wait! What about uncle Giovanni?

Ernesto shrugged. Since Bernardo had told him,
laughing the while, the story of the treacherous shave
(for which he offered to pay and was accepted), uncle
Giovanni had not tried to lay a hand on him, not even
to convince him by the head-clouting method that the
socialists were wrong. Now he accepted him as a man,
and he hardly spoke to him. He still gave him the florin
after Sunday lunch (nearly always fish, which the uncle
was very partial to and Ernesto detested) but did not
want to argue about politics; until one day he took the
opportunity presented by a scandal in the city in-
volving a well-known public figure who apparently
had the same urges as the labourer and had released

them on — and under — a young servant boy (*in both directions*, as his political opponents were quick to stress), to fix him with a beady eye and a levelled forefinger and say: There's nothing left for a man who has done that but to shoot himself — if he *is* a man.

He's talking just like the other one, thought Ernesto; he went on about drowning himself for shame, and now this about shooting people. But Ernesto was (at that time, still) glad to be alive; he had no intention of shooting himself over such a little thing . . . Nor for that matter did the member of parliament shoot himself: he fell victim to a crusade by the *austriacanti*, the Austrophiles (there were many in Trieste, not all of them time-servers, and they published their own newspaper) and made do with hopping to another continent (easily done in those days). But his uncle's words, and even more his firm gaze (as if he knew everything or at least suspected it) stuck in his memory, and were perhaps not the least cause of the inevitable but sudden break with the man. He was more and more afraid of his uncle, and if he shrugged now at the mention of his name, it was really to shake off this fear.

Are you going, mother?

Signora Celestina took her son's impatience as proof that he wanted to settle his differences with Signor Wilder. She heaved a sigh and said as she left the room to change her dress:

I'll do what I can, but don't expect too much. It all depends on that letter you wrote. Be careful not to wake your aunt, and for the time being . . . thank you so much. With this Parthian shot she did what Ernesto wanted just then more than anything else: she left the room, and minutes later the house. Only after he had heard her softly close the front door, so not to disturb her sister, did he remember the crucial item: the half month's pay Signor Wilder had promised to give her. But he knew how scrupulous he was in money matters; what was more doubtful was whether his own 'lady mother' would pass on the third share he was due. Intuition warned him to expect the worst.

Stirred from her slumber by a request for money from someone she thought should have been at work, his aunt flatly refused — *You ought to be in bed if you're ill, not going to the theatre* — and went straight back to sleep. Ernesto threw himself on to the famous brass bed, just as the old lady had advised, but not to nurse his illness (which if it existed at all, would not be cured by staying in bed). He needed to think over the whole situation.

Blast my impatience! he thought. I'm *sure* she would have given me the money if only I'd waited till she woke up. For a few kind words I could be going to Ondricek tonight. But now — he sighed deeply, just as his mother had done — now I've wrecked my life forever.

All my mother's fault too, he went on, muttering to himself. She's the one who took me away from school and sent me to that damned Signor Wilder, who can go to hell. Mulling over his schooldays he skipped the senior school, which still haunted him on account of a teacher who had persecuted him — unfairly, he was still sure — with bad marks, and concentrated instead on the Imperial Royal Academy of Commerce and Nautical Science, where his mother enrolled him when he graduated from the senior school, and where he only completed the first term of the first year. In the days of Franz Josef II, the commercial department at the Academy was the only sphere of public life (except for the parliament, riven by nationalist hatreds) which openly and stubbornly refused to function; nobody took it seriously, neither the students nor the teachers. After the hard grind of the senior school Ernesto had a whale of a time at the Academy, where he rounded off the 'education' begun by his corrupt cousin — even the proper lessons were usually a bedlam by the end. (*Bedlam* is euphemistic: what with the displaying of penises and other sideshows of the sort, those classrooms were truly infernal.) Once again, as at the junior school, he was at or near the top in every subject except German, which he always found difficult. But his mother was not happy with this way of studying, or rather not-studying.

Ernesto, have you finished your homework already? she used to ask at least once a day.

Of course, mummy, he would answer from the brass bed, engrossed in a book borrowed from his cousin or bought with his uncle's weekly present. If she persisted he would get up, annoyed but willing, and show her his exercise books, although they looked more disgraceful by the day. But his mother was unconvinced; even his teachers' good reports (they were amazed and even grateful to be taken seriously for once) could not persuade her. While the son enjoyed the Academy enormously it certainly didn't suit the mother, and she decided to look for work on his behalf (without telling him first) as soon as he could apply for jobs without needing to have finished at the Academy; she would take him away from there the very day she found something suitable. (Perhaps too she needed to be less dependent on her sister, at least where her son was concerned, for he was a big boy now.) So it was that Ernesto found himself in Signor Wilder's office one morning, where an apprentice was just what they wanted. His mother was there too, with a letter of introduction from an old friend (one Signora Sarina, known as 'Sarina de la Pasta' because she owned a macaroni shop near the market). Ernesto made a good (i.e. honest) impression and was engaged on the spot: for a trial period, of course, and without pay for the first six months. He was fifteen years old and — so his mother believed, anyway — as pure as the driven snow.

All her fault, he muttered again, gripped with nostalgia for school and envy of his old schoolmates, who all seemed better and luckier than he. (Such were the boys who had advanced from the junior to the senior school and soon had to face the terrifying final examinations; and such the ones still merrymaking for the last year at the Academy of Commerce.) He took a book from the little bedside table and, to banish this nostalgia, began to sketch a caricature of his old Italian teacher on the endpapers, as he had often done at the Academy. What a donkey, he murmured as he drew, even more of a donkey than that donkey which used to carry vegetables to the corner shop every morning with the old white-bearded gardener prodding him along (the gardener had what his school primer called 'a Patriarch's beard'), and wake the whole house with its braying. Anyway his features are so unmistakable and easy to do that sailors can even see them on the walls at the Cape of Good Hope, thanks to his old students from the nautical science department. Ernesto's caricature was just as good as the other boys' used to be (if not better), but this time the exercise only deepened his melancholy. He tore the cover off the book when the drawing was still unfinished, ripped it up, and threw the pieces as far across the room as he could — as once with the shreds of the superfine flour label and later with the birch wand the man had cut to 'punish' him. When she saw the mess Signora Celestina would grumble and clear it up.

Now he was longing for her to come back, hoping she would give him his share of the money. Then at least he could go to the concert that night and have a little fun . . . But even if he did have fun tonight, what next? . . . Could I go back to school? he wondered. If I work on my own for a while and sit the exam, I could join in the eighth grade. (He was no longer considering a business career, nor even the delightful Academy: now — sad sign! — he felt the need for austerity.) But he realized how difficult it would be even to try; he would need money to pay for private lessons — his aunt would have to foot the bill, and she was so mean; and his mother would make all sorts of other difficulties. He even considered writing off the last three years at the Academy and the office, using his promotional certificate (it must still be somewhere in the house — but where?) to enrol in the fifth grade. Wouldn't he cut a fine figure sitting next to fourteen- and fifteen-year-olds, and him seventeen! They would all think he was one of those boys (he'd scorned them too in his time) who are forever repeating grades. Everyone would pick on me from the start, he thought; I'd stick out like a sore thumb. And then . . . did he have the *right* to go back to school, to *sit* on those benches again after what he had done? At this thought (a rather idiotic one, the reader must admit) he leaped off the bed as if pricked by a thorn — or was it a snakebite?

Remorse is our deluded vision of a past episode: we remember the action and forget the emotions which brought it about, the blazing air that shaped whatever happened and made it inevitable. Seen as a bald fact, this can easily seem monstrous, and thus it was (because he reviewed it in a false light) that Ernesto remembered his relationship with the man: words,

acts, everything now took a different colour to what it
had had in the flowing reality of life. He was also
thinking he should say a frank and proper farewell to
the man: should tell him he had wanted to resign from
Signor Wilder's business, not leave him simply feeling
betrayed. Towards the end, after the affair had become
oppressive and finally intolerable, there was a trace of
fear in his feeling for him. We remarked before that the
man and uncle Giovanni were the only people in the
world he was afraid of; we can add that just now he was
more afraid of the man. What if he told someone, to
get revenge for the desertion which must seem so
unfair to him? And went into detail, and laughed at
him? Mightn't he tell Cesco, for instance? They were
certainly friends; Cesco was often drunk, what's more,
and drunks can't keep their mouths shut — they'll say
anything about themselves and anybody else. Not the
man — he never drank, or hardly ever — he only had
one bad habit . . . But how well did he know him? To
judge by their conversations (which were actually
more like monologues) he was a good man, all in all, if
rather obsessed in some ways, and surely incapable of
deliberately hurting anyone. But (and needless to say,
there was no hint of disdain in Ernesto's comparison)
he came from such a different class and background
. . . What if they ever met in the street by chance and
the man seized him, even upbraided him in public? At
this moment the poor boy was more 'a boy' than ever,
and even more mistaken now than a few days before,
when he was drinking in the tree-lined piazza and
utterly misjudged the young women's laughter. The
man had good reasons of his own to be more afraid of
Ernesto than Ernesto was of him, and he not only
never confided in a soul (his attitude towards a boy
who brought him pleasure and not for money, was —
if one may so put it — chivalrous), but the few times

they met in the street he pretended not to see him. This
first happened as he was taking Cesco home one day,
when the fat man was so drunk his legs would not
carry him; the other encounters were many years later,
at ever greater intervals. Ernesto was much changed
himself and barely recognized him: could not be quite
sure it wasn't somebody else. With his hands clasped
behind his bent back, he looked like an old man — a
feeble old man, even a beggar (which he was not).
Their eyes met each time; each time both men looked
away, and never a word was said. It was over, finished
for good. Ernesto only wanted to forget everything
now, only wanted to look forward to the concert with
a light heart — the concert he knew he would hear,
somehow or other . . .


Ernesto's first words were *Did you get the money,
mother*? when she was barely over the threshold.
Breathing hard after the climb upstairs (they lived on
the fifth storey of a house at the edge of the old city),
she did not speak for a minute. The question seemed
inappropriate, to say the least, and not at all what she
was expecting. She thought her son would want —
more than want: would be agog — to know the outcome of her interview with Signor Wilder. Although
her face remained as sober and serious as her dress (she
always wore black when she went out), it did not, in
truth, betoken such terrible news.

For all his impatience to know whether or not he
could go to the concert, Ernesto let the poor woman sit
down and catch her breath. Then he asked what Signor
Wilder had said.

Signor Wilder is an angel, replied his mother. You
don't deserve his goodness. I read the letter you wrote;
indeed he very graciously offered to read it to me

himself.

This was not what Ernesto wanted to hear: he knew the letter by heart. All the same, he asked her what she thought of it.

Already knowing the gist, Signora Celestina had actually been expecting the tone of the letter to be much more offensive and the language much worse than they were. But she still expressed her full disapproval (it being an article of faith with her that you can never show sons enough disapproval).

I think what Signor Wilder quite rightly thinks: it's a rude letter, written by a bad boy. As I listened to him reading I couldn't recognize my son at all.

But why wouldn't he give me money for the tram? I'd like to see him tramping the streets all day in this weather.

Signor Wilder is still young, but he's a few years older than you, and anyway he says he didn't refuse you the money: he only thought it was costing too much for a healthy boy like — here Signora Celestina secretly crossed her fingers to ward off any lurking evil spirits — like you, thank the Lord. And he told me you insisted on going out yourself and never let the new apprentice go instead.

Did you see him? asked Ernesto, perking up. What did you think?

Signora Celestina had a jealous heart, at least where her son was concerned, and she had not warmed to the new apprentice. She immediately judged him to be a hypocrite — which he was. At the same time she did not want to set Ernesto against him; she was under the illusion that she had put everything right (half of it, anyway); so her son really should be able to live with him for a few hours a day. She deflected his question.

This is what Signor Wilder proposes, she went on. It was very difficult for me to arrange (not true: the idea

had come spontaneously from the 'exploiter' of
Ernesto's legs, and his mother told this little lie to
heighten the drama and make the most of her own
part in it) but Signor Wilder is truly a good person and
it was a lucky day when my friend Signora Sarina
thought of him. She couldn't have chosen better for a
boy like you.

I don't understand, Ernesto interrupted, beginning
to understand, alas! and fearing the worst. You talk as
if I'm going back to the office tomorrow.

Not tomorrow and maybe never. There's no use
complaining; we have to live with our mistakes.
Signor Wilder is giving you a whole week's paid
holiday, for you to relax, he says, and look after yourself. Then he is ready to take you back, at half-pay
certainly, and for half-days' work: mornings or afternoons, as you prefer. He's expecting a reply tomorrow
and will square the accounts with you then himself. It
will be enough for him if you manage the Italian
correspondence, which he says you do very well.

And, mother, did — did you accept?

As I said, he'll be waiting for your reply tomorrow.
He was quite clear that if you show you're sorry about
that stupid letter — though you won't have to *say*
anything — and prove your goodwill, he'll take you
back full-time as before. Meanwhile he will pay for the
work you do; that means fifteen instead of thirty
crowns a month.

Ernesto had flung himself on the brass bed; he lay
there now as he had lain there reading *The Arabian
Nights* in that vanished, never-to-be-repeated
summer. Then he had been happy; now he was in
despair. He was (unfairly, he recognized) angry with
his mother too, who for her part could not have begun
to guess the 'real reason' why he'd had himself sacked
by Signor Wilder. The scheme he had devised and

brought to fruition — or so he'd thought! — was made
wasted effort by this proposal. His house of cards
collapsed. Even if he went back to the office only for
the mornings, or only the afternoons, he would be sure
to meet the man. How could he tell his mother? How
could he make her understand? At that moment — like
Faust when the condemned Margarita refuses to be led
out of prison to safety, choosing to stay for the
executioner — he asked himself, for the first time in his
life, *Why was I ever born*? (He had just read the first part
of the poem in a pocket edition published, as ever, by
Sonzogno in, predictably, a stolid prose translation;
and had recently seen a performance of Arrigo Boito's
*Mephistopheles*, which was all the rage then, like
*Ischirogeno*.) But the same moment brought fresh inspiration, either from above or from below. He knew
the only thing that was left to do and decided to do it,
whatever the cost:

I'm not going back to Signor Wilder.

Signora Celestina was slightly taken aback by the
resolution in her son's voice but still thought it was a
question of resentment, or injured pride, or something
of that sort. He won't tell you off, she said, he
promised not to, and he made it clear he'll raise your
pay at the end of the year if everything returns to
normal. He was thinking of doing so anyway before
you wrote the letter. He spoke like a father, she added,
not like an employer at all, let alone an employer who
has been wrongfully insulted. No one else in your
position . . .

I shan't set foot in Signor Wilder's office again, not
even if he begs my pardon and raises the pay to a
hundred crowns a month.

Signora Celestina was incensed.

You are a bad son, she said, and a worthless creature.
You're just like your father, you're determined to kill

me with worry. She did not cry: merely rose from the chair she had slumped into, panting, after climbing the stairs, and went to the door.

Don't go, Ernesto said in a voice suddenly soft, almost imploring. Mother, there's something I have to confess, and it may make you unhappy but I *must* tell you. When you know what it is you won't keep insisting I go back to Signor Wilder. Mother — he started, but dried up at once. How could he *say* it? How could he tell his mother? A boy who liked to speak his mind, as Ernesto did, could talk openly to someone like the labourer — but to his mother? . . . He had decided to tell her the entire story as soon as he knew Signor Wilder's proposal. Apart from his own predicament at the moment, perhaps he was just too young to bear his 'terrible' secret alone; he needed to confide in someone, as the man had feared he would, and whom should he trust if not his mother? True, she was a dour woman, more often than not unable to understand him, but she was still his mother. And how else could he escape going back to the office? Unless he gave her the 'real' reason for his refusal, he foresaw worse scenes than if he confessed everything, and what's more there would be no end to them. His heart was in his mouth; he was a bit sorry for the man as well: telling their story was a second betrayal. But he could trust his mother never to tell a soul. The difficulty lay in finding the words . . .

Signora Celestina was seated again, waiting for her son to speak. Her heart too was beating fast; she was expecting something serious, and did not feel strong enough to survive another blow, she had suffered so much in her life.

Tell me, she said. It was almost a command. Her own ideas were a thousand miles off the mark.

But Ernesto still said nothing. He still couldn't find

the words, and stayed where he was on the bed, his head bowed in his hands.

His mother was more and more alarmed. You haven't — she began in a hushed voice, looking round as if for eavesdroppers, though no one else was in the room or in the rooms adjacent — you haven't stolen any money from Signor Wilder, have you? She knew her son was honest, but he was a spendthrift too, and one was always reading in the papers about the incredible things that boys of Ernesto's age and younger did, who only the day before had seemed like little cherubs. Of all the 'crimes' poor people can commit, theft distressed her most.

No, mother, I haven't stolen anything.

Then what have you done? In God's name say what it is, stop torturing me!

Now theft was ruled out (she knew Ernesto did not lie to her) she sensed that something much less serious was at issue. She was thinking (and perhaps was not far wrong) of some nonsense or other, some boyish game which her son took too seriously. For she knew he was an exaggerator as well as a spendthrift.

My son, she said, unwittingly making his confession more bitter, you can't have done anything so very shameful that you can't tell your mother without blushing. Here I am, and I'm listening.

Ernesto had found the words.

Do you remember that man who came to the house one day when I was ill? He wanted the bills which I'd forgotten in my jacket pocket. Signor Wilder sent him . . .

The labourer? You mean the man you told me to fetch a glass of wine for? He didn't seem a bad type to me. But I don't understand . . .

I know you can't understand yet, and maybe — maybe you won't understand afterwards, but I must tell you all the same. Do you remember, he continued, lowering his voice, what uncle Giovanni told me one Sunday after lunch, before he gave me the florin? When there was that blasted scandal about the member of parliament in all the newspapers? It wasn't long ago. *There's nothing left for a man who's done that but to shoot himself*, he said. Well, mother, mummy, we did that, the man and I . . .

Albeit for different reasons Signora Celestina could remember her brother's exact words at the end of that meal. A magnificent poached sea bass had been served — a gift from the guest, for whom she had spent the whole morning carefully preparing a lavish mayonnaise sauce. She also remembered that her son had been disturbed — *because*, she thought at the time, *he's too delicate*; so noticeably disturbed, in fact, that she was a bit angry with her brother for bringing the subject up at dinnertime. She supposed he did it 'for educational reasons', but there was no real need in Ernesto's case: he was a model of innocence, or seemed so to her. For that matter she had only a vague notion of what *that* was; she believed it to be the exclusive prerogative of the 'servant class' — like dialect — and had never really been convinced that a personage of distinction, a member of parliament no less, would sully himself like that; it must have been his enemies' plotting. He was a gentleman, after all; and despite his poverty and his dependence on the aunt, Ernesto was a gentleman too.

Don't ask any questions, Ernesto begged, shielding his face with his hands, peering through his fingers at his mother and reading the dismay in her eyes. He was afraid he had dealt a mortal blow, would see her tumble from her chair any moment now, murdered by her own son . . . Had he not been so distraught himself, he would have noticed that his words came almost as a relief to his mother. He had been so anxious that she was expecting something even worse.

Now you understand why I can't go back to Signor Wilder: I mustn't see that man again.

Signora Celestina was blind to everything but the physical dimension of the affair, and more than anything else this simply baffled her. The significance, the psychological motive, utterly escaped her; otherwise she would have had to understand that her mistaken marriage, the total absence of a father, and her own needless severity had each played a part . . . even making no allowance for Ernesto's age and, what was more important, for his singular 'grace', which may have sprung from those very same deprivations.

Villain! she cried, pouncing on the man. Blackguard! Murderer! He's worse than your . . . Abusing a boy like that! I'll find him, don't worry, and I'll have something to tell him when I do. He should jump into the sea for shame at the very sight of me, and he'd better too if he doesn't want me to . . .

No, said Ernesto, it's not all his fault, and if you don't want to make trouble for me too, swear never to look for him or see him or talk to him. Because, mother, you don't know . . . It's over now, but if I go back to Signor Wilder . . . He said he loved me and he never let me alone . . . He even bought me cakes.

And you want me to let him go scot-free after what he's done to my son, to a respectable boy . . .

I'm not respectable any more, and I'm not a boy any more either, Ernesto said despite himself, or not legally anyway. And if I hadn't wanted . . .

You're not going to tell me you asked him?

No, mother, not asked him, no, but . . . but I met him more than halfway. That's why you mustn't say anything to anyone, least of all uncle Giovanni. (For it had occurred to him as the worst possibility of all that his mother might report the affair to his uncle, who was also his guardian and, Ernesto was sure, half-mad into the bargain . . . Ernesto's father had been exiled from the Austrian empire for irredentist subversion; for with Venice lost, Trieste was Austria's 'fairest jewel'; every minor who had been deprived of paternal support by death or misadventure was legally required to have a guardian, if only *pro forma*.)

Swear not to breathe a word of this to uncle Giovanni. You must swear, mummy. If you don't . . . He began to cry.

This time, miraculously, Signora Celestina understood that her son needed cherishing more than scolding. The affair disgusted her, needless to say, but more than that it was, as we said, simply beyond her. She did not make it a matter of life and death, as Ernesto was scared she might; it would be enough for her if it was kept absolutely secret, so that no one, not even the breeze, knew or suspected a thing.

But him — that man — are you certain he won't talk about it?

Certain, Ernesto forced himself to lie.

Nor must you tell a soul, not even your cousin, woe betide you! You know the sort of boy he is. (She was worried her son might be a gossip as well as an exaggerator and a spendthrift.)

Did he hurt you very much? she added quietly.

Oh mother! begged Ernesto, burying his head deeper in his arms. Just then his corrupt cousin seemed the very pattern of virtue.

Oh my boy, my poor boy! — Signora Celestina melted. This time she followed her heart; she sent morality and its abject homilies to the devil (i.e. back to their true father), bent over her boy, and kissed his face.

You must swear never to do it again, she said. It is an ugly, indecent thing (Ernesto could not help but be reminded of the 'style' of his school essays, which had brought him the teacher's hostility) and unworthy of a fine boy like you. Only those urchins who sell lemonade at streetcorners in Rena Vecchia do that, not my Pimpo . . . (In her rare expansive moods Signora Celestina called her son by the name he gave the black-bird.)

After his mother's kiss, sensing forgiveness was at hand, Ernesto felt reborn. It was one of very few kisses she had ever given him: the poor woman set such store on being — and even more on being seen to be – a 'Spartan mother'.

Don't think about it any more, she said, suddenly and unwittingly speaking dialect, which was another rare event. What happened to you is very bad, my son, but so long as no one knows it isn't so very important. You're not a child any longer, thank God.

I'm not a child at all, Ernesto protested, I've been with a woman too.

And he burst into tears, just as he had done some six or seven years before when he read *Cuore* by Edmondo De Amicis for the first time. He sobbed lustily.

Perhaps he thought he could wash away the first confession with the second one, but this time his mother's jealous soul was more deeply hurt. Where her son was concerned, she was, like the man, though from different (or partly different) motives, frightened of women: of streetwalkers because of diseases, and of the rest for other reasons.

But, she said, I thought you were still pure as the driven snow.

Her answer was a moan from the brass bed, the moan of a stabbed man.

That's enough now, said Signora Celestina, getting

to her feet. What's done is done. I'll speak to Signor
Wilder and tell him you're not well, or find another
excuse without lying to him. You won't have to see
them again, neither Signor Wilder nor . . . the other
one.

Do you mean it, mother? Am I forgiven? — Ernesto
wanted a second kiss but did not dare to ask.

I've already forgiven you, said Signora Celestina.
Now up and out with you, you mustn't lie here
moping.

Ernesto sat up on the bed. His tear-washed hazel
eyes shone like a light of childish goodness.

Mother, he said, there's a concert tonight and I so
want to go to it: Ondricek is playing, the violinist, you
know the one, I heard him last year and liked him very
much. I told you about him, don't you remember?

You're still obsessed by the violin, aren't you, replied Signora Celestina, as a fond mother today might
tell her sporty son *You're football-mad* when he's
threatening to slip away from his books or his work.

Yes, mother, but that's not why I'm . . . If Signor
Wilder had given you the fortnight's pay he owes me, I
could have asked you for . . .

Now she understood the reason for that first
question, which had seemed so untimely, as soon as
she came in. She understood, and she might even have
smiled if she had not been so unhappy. She sighed
instead, took a handkerchief (hers was coloured too)
from a pocket inside her dress, and untied the knot.

How much is a ticket?

Two florins, mummy, he said, not daring to believe
what he heard and saw. (The price he quoted was for a
seat; he did not like listening on his feet, and it wasn't
strictly a lie.)

She handed him the florins, which he pocketed. Just
then he would have given anything (except a concert

ticket) to spare her the least anxiety. He had no idea that the poor woman managed to do a little work of her own, known only to herself, so that she would not have to depend completely on her sister: wretched little deals in brokerage, or something similar. Ernesto had never asked how she came by the bit of money which she spent largely on him — sons are egoists, as everyone knows.

Mother, he said in a strange voice, that childish light in his eyes even brighter now the clouds had dispersed and he was sure of going to the concert — Mother, can I ask you something?

(This was his famous *Can I?* Ernesto adored asking questions, and adored asking permission to ask them.)

What?

You don't have to answer if you don't want, mummy . . . Can I?

Ask me, said Signora Celestina uneasily.

Was my father, came the timid question, really *so* bad?

Don't ask about him, his mother said, as if touched on the quick of a wound. He was a murderer, that's what he was, that's what he was to me. That, my son, is all you need to know . . .

But . . . but what did he do to you?

Signora Celestina did not answer her son's artless question directly.

When you were little, she said, and living with your nanny, I spent every night alone and very sick in this room. Do you see the clock over there? (pointing to an old clock with little alabaster columns, which still told the time in the bedroom with the sloping roof, where Ernesto now slept) I listened to it every night, *had* to listen to it, and its tick tock seemed to be telling me over and over again *Alone, alone, always alone.* That's how I spent my nights, alone and very sick, and it was your father's fault. There was no one to help me. In those days your aunt . . . You were in the country with your beloved nanny . . .

Oh mother! cried Ernesto, and he jumped up to hug her. But she drew back, almost pushing him away: one kiss was all very well, but two . . .

Now get changed, she said, if you don't want to be late for the concert. And don't ring the bell when you come back — knock gently, I'll be waiting up for you and I'll hear. Do be careful not to wake your aunt. That is all I ask.

## Almost an Ending

This, clearly, is not the young Ernesto's whole story, only that of the Ernesto who for good reasons or bad has himself sacked by Signor Wilder, then confesses everything to his mother and is forgiven by her, and is now, thanks to her gift of two florins, about to leave for the concert he's so keen to hear, by the violinist Ondricek.

What follows — the 'fateful' meeting at the concert, which in turn begets another, yet more 'fateful' one — would suffice for another hundred pages at least; add Ernesto's discovery of his 'vocation' and the real story of his adolescence would indeed be complete. Unfortunately the author is too old, too weary, and too embittered to feel able to write those pages. Yet there is no need to despair of the future — or so he tells himself; *There are no lost wars, only victories postponed*: an incorrigible optimist/activist was once brave enough to utter these words in his hearing. So he leaves a door ajar for the hopes of his few friends (very few — no more than three or four, so I've heard, including that dangerous activist). They are the only people for whom he 'risked' this story; they have loved Ernesto and understood his failings and his grace, and — if they think its worthwhile — they can look forward to the day when the author will find the inner strength (and outward conditions) to press on and perhaps even reach the end of his story.

Trieste, 31 August 1953

# Fifth Episode

Franz Ondricek (born in Prague, 1859; collapsed and died at Milan railway station, 1922) possessed qualities which set him not only apart from the other violinists who performed at Trieste in those years, but — in some people's judgement, including Ernesto's — above them. He played not at the Schiller Club (where the German colony met) but at the Music Society, which was an Italian, indeed an irredentist circle (perhaps this was why Ondricek preferred it, for he himself was a Bohemian nationalist); nor did he play standing up, with medals gleaming on his lapel. He did not even play without a score; obviously he knew the pieces he *pretended* to read no less well than his compeers, but to cut a dash and assert a style of his own he played sitting down, like a member of a quartet, the music open on a stand before him and a bespectacled young man alert at his side: probably his favourite pupil — thought Ernesto — who accompanied him on all his travels to turn the pages of his score. Ondricek's audience that year was smaller than usual, because he had arrived very late in the season. (He came to Trieste almost every year and usually filled half the auditorium, two-thirds at most; but it should be remembered that the Music Society's premises were bigger than those of the Schiller Club.) Ernesto was one of the first to enter and take his seat (in the third row: near the front but not too near) and he had a while to wait before the concert began. He was still overwrought and excited by the scene with his mother and the unexpected joy of the outcome. She's not nearly as bad as she wants people to think, my mother, he thought, partly in gratitude and partly to hum himself a lullaby. He was glad he had confessed and been forgiven, and that with her forgiveness she had given him the money to buy a seat at the concert. And even gladder not to be going back to Signor Wilder the next morning and all the mornings after that. His own tears had worked on him like medicine; for the moment he did not worry what he was going to do with his life. He scanned the hall to see if his employer (a keen concert-goer, he knew) was in the audience; but no sign of him. Signor Wilder would like to have heard Ondricek play, but he had 'solid political reasons' for never darkening the doors of the Music Society.

For Ondricek as for all his rivals, having an effect on his audience was more important than anything else; but his programmes were more serious, more 'classical' than theirs, and rightly or wrongly Ernesto was sure that Ondricek was one of the greatest living musicians. That night, what's more, straining not to miss a single note, he heard him play Bach's famous *Chaconne* for solo violin, which people extolled as the ultimate in chamber music. Ernesto never suspected that even Ondricek included it in his repertoire above all for the technical challenge to his skill, and because of the audience's delight at seeing someone perform both theme and accompaniment on one instrument. The applause for the *Chaconne* was warmer than ever, and in the third row (near the front but not too near) Ernesto clapped till his hands were glowing. (You would have thought he was protesting at something, not cheering it.) It even seemed to him that Ondricek noticed his youthful fervour and returned a faint smile of thanks: almost a smile of farewell.

The *Chaconne* concluded the first part of the programme. There was a ten-minute interval; to make it pass more quickly Ernesto decided to promenade around the hall with the rest of the audience, though unlike the rest (who were nearly all adults of a more-than-certain age) he had no acquaintances to greet, no lady to bow before and kiss her hand, as people did in those days. It was during this promenade that fate waylaid him for the second time, and pushed him — as before — in a wrong direction.

Beside one of the large gilt mirrors adorning the walls of the Music Society stood a boy, his arms folded across his chest. He was alone. He wore short trousers, though he was a little too old for them, and his blond hair fell down to his shoulders (this being another fashion of the time, especially among artists, real or bogus; we still remember a certain learned man, very well-known in the city and even beyond, whose fame and honours were in great part due to his long hair, which he preserved well into old age, sparse and straggly though it was). Gazing straight ahead, the boy seemed lost in thought — about what we could not say, but it certainly excluded present company, including Ernesto. It must have been a happy thought too: he was smiling — as the saying goes — *at the angels*. He was very handsome indeed. Ernesto knew at first sight that he was a violin student, a future concert artist who would in time outshine all the rest. He stood quite still, watching him, until the bell announced the second half of the concert. Ernesto waited to see where the prodigy was sitting, hoping there might be an empty place beside him. But the boy had a complimentary ticket for 'standing room only' and he stayed where he was, his gaze still fixed on that vision known to himself alone; it was as if Ondricek and his concert scarcely existed. Sensing someone's eyes riveted on him, he glanced in Ernesto's direction for a second, but

apparently without seeing him. (We say *apparently*
because he knew very well he was being looked at —
looked at, what's more, by someone in love with him.)
That's that, thought Ernesto, I'm rejected out of hand.
Realizing the boy was not going to move, he returned
to his seat in the third row, but returned as a different
person, changed more in two minutes than by the past
ten years. He kept having to stop himself turning to
look at the marvel, for he did not want people to notice
him. (No one was paying him or the marvel any
attention whatever.) The emotions stirred in his soul
were various and complicated, and the result was an
ache, a despondency, such as he had never felt before.

First there was envy. It was not bad envy (which
wants to take simply for the pleasure of taking) but
rather envy born of the desire, as passionate as it was
hopeless, to *be* like its object. Of course he's a born
violinist, he said to himself, who's fired by an irresistible vocation (which is joyfully accepted by everyone around him), and he began taking lessons when he
was only five, and he's destined for the most amazing
triumphs pretty soon (like Kubelik's, maybe even
greater). His teacher wasn't still tuning *his* violin after
two years, that's for sure. (And he laughed inwardly,
but it was hollow laughter.)

Perhaps he was studying for the final or penultimate
grade at a famous faraway conservatoire, under the
expert eye of an old maestro — he had long hair too,
but his was completely white — who admitted he had
no more to teach this extraordinary pupil who was
both his pride and his hope for the future. He only
came home to Trieste for the holidays, blessing his
beloved parents with his company, and perhaps even
deigned to enjoy himself like any other boy his age —
forgetting his glorious future for a few hours a day, yet
always knowing that if he had brought his violin with

him (a Stradivarius, of course, given by an anonymous
admirer), he could have bewitched everyone on the
beach at the first sweep of his bow. Look how he's
dressed! he went on, torturing himself; his parents love
him so much, they want him to stay a boy forever:
they can't bring themselves to put him in long
trousers. (The boy was wearing short trousers reluctantly, to save his parents' money.) What good care
they must take of him, looking after him and keeping
him close by, as close as possible . . . like a rose to their
cheeks. (They certainly were very fond of him at home
— especially his mother — but had had enough of his
'airs and graces'; they — especially his father — wanted
him to have a haircut and start training to play in an
orchestra as soon as possible, so he would be off their
hands, financially at least.) These envious thoughts
were joined by other, self-reproachful ones: *That* boy
could never find himself having to confess to his
mother what I confessed today. You only need look at
him to know he's never stooped to that, not with
women or men. (If they had been friends Ernesto
would soon have known that, finding himself alone
and out of sight in the country one day, he had even
stooped — like the shepherds of antiquity — with a
little goat: *and* he had bragged about it.) He doesn't
think I'm even worth speaking to: oh how contemptuous he is of me! how . . . (As if, just now, Ernesto
needed anyone's help in contempt of himself.) Added
to this self-denigration (standard with adolescent
lovers, after all, even in normal cases) was the desire to
know the boy and make him return his admiration.
But what was he supposed to admire? Well, if that
much was impossible he would make the other boy
accept *his* admiration; would live at his side — live with
him and help him (as if he needed any help!); would be,
in a word, his *best friend*. But here Ernesto knew that

his wounded heart — wounded by beauty, and for the first time — gave the word *friend* an intensity outside its usual scope, and this knowledge only made him more despondent.

Meanwhile Ondricek had almost reached the end of the last work in his programme — the last before the numerous obligatory encores, without which the evening would be counted a moral failure. It was Paganini's *Perpetual Motion*, for this and not the Bach *Chaconne* was his 'trusty warhorse', as the phrase went, and people say that his rendition was unsurpassed. Ernesto scarcely heard it. He left his seat before the end, wanting to be sure he saw the marvellous boy again on the way out, for if he could not *be* he would make do with *having*. If I find him, he thought, I'll stop him: I can ask him if he plays the violin himself and what he thought of Ondricek tonight. After all, he added to cheer himself up, he's a boy too, and only a bit younger than me. Following one of those famous inspirations (from above or from below) he would have stopped him too. But he searched in vain; the boy had either left already or, tired of standing, found an empty seat. The possibility that *that* boy had been standing all the time because he could not afford to sit down never crossed his mind. He could not find him anywhere, seated or standing: as if the sweet, tormenting vision had taken wing! The fact was, he had already, unwillingly, left the hall; he lived some distance away in the hills behind the city, had no money for the tram, and wanted to avoid the scolding which followed whenever he arrived home late. Like Signora Celestina, his mother did not yet trust her son with the house keys, and when he went out in the evening she waited up for him or persuaded his sister to do so. (She was the younger of the two by a year; they were as like as two pins, and the boy was so possessively devoted to her that he once wanted to beat her — as if she'd have let him, the little thug! — when he thought she was flirting too much with one of his friends. He had quite a few friends, and they were all 'geniuses' like him: all destined to change the world somehow or other, all more or less in love with his sister Luigia.) Who on earth can he be? wondered Ernesto, peering desperately around, convinced that if he lost him this time he would never see him again. How handsome he was! Very confident, very proud . . . too proud, maybe. Where can this strange, marvellous boy have come from? What can his name be? . . . He did not realize that they had met and he had already been very envious of him four years before, as he lay on the brass bed in that other, happier, less eventful summer . . . Whatever his name here and now in Trieste, this strange, marvellous boy was the confectioner's son in Baghdad (or was it in Basra?), the boy who accepted one, yes, and even two sherbet ices, but repulsed the good host's caresses with a shake of his head and the words *Stay where you are. Be content to watch and serve me.*

One evening Ernesto and Ilio were walking down the delectable hill of Scorcola. They wanted to go for a swim, although it was late.

A young woman was climbing the road towards them. She was tall, and she carried herself proudly. She wasn't 'beautiful': her hair was corn gold, swept up in a pyramid so that she appeared even taller; her eyes were an indefinable colour, with a slight squint. No, she wasn't beautiful — she was something else. The two boys looked at her, then at each other.

What do you think? asked Ilio.

She's the fall of Troy, Ernesto answered, partly in Italian, partly in dialect. He was reading Virgil for the first time, and was enthralled. But he had spoken rather too loudly.

The woman with the regal bearing half-heard his reply, did not understand the tribute, and looked round indignantly, muttering *Bloody kids* under her breath.

The reader will have gathered straightaway that Ilio was the boy Ernesto had found and lost at Ondricek's concert. Lost, then rediscovered the next day when they met face to face on the steps outside their violin teacher's room. As it turned out they had been sharing the same teacher since the begining of the week.

At first they pretended not to see one another, but Ernesto's heart was beating too fast and too hard: he could not stop himself: after a few steps he looked back, to find that the other boy had turned too. His hour's lesson just finished (he had three per week), he was making way for the next pupil, who happened to be Ernesto. They looked at each other for a moment, saying nothing; then they came closer, as if propelled by a force beyond their control. They looked like two young dogs, except that they smiled instead of wagging their tails.

What's your name? — Ernesto was the first to speak.

The godlike boy was in long trousers (he had to wear them alternately with the shorts so they would last longer) and seemed more human; there was none of the haughtiness of the previous evening, and Ernesto liked him all the more. He told Ernesto his surname, which could hardly be of interest to the reader.

And your first name?

Emilio, but everyone calls me Ilio. And you?

He had just said *lei*, which Ernesto did not like; it

underlined the age difference, which must have been small but could not be ignored.

Mine's Ernesto . . . But Ilio, why do you call me *lei*? How old are you?

Fifteen and a half.

I'm seventeen, just. If you like we can still use *tu* and our first names.

Yes, let's! Ilio smiled. I only said *lei* because I'd never spoken to you before. Are you learning the violin too? He nodded at the instrument case; they were both holding them, like elegant little suitcases. Ernesto was pleased, of course, but somewhat uneasy at the same time, and he parried the question with another:

Have you been learning for long?

Not so long really — I only started when I was thirteen. That's late, don't you think?

And here his mobile nose came into its own; which is to say, he wrinkled it in what was to Ernesto a quite inimitable way. Now it was an unconscious habit, but at school he used to do it in exchange for a pen nib, or better still a bright glass marble.

For a moment Ernesto was speechless. Then he said, I started when I was fifteen, but you . . . you must be very good.

Why d'you think that? (Ilio was hoping their teacher had said so, but while the teacher was satisfied with him, wanting only a little more discipline and application, he never discussed his pupils favourably or otherwise. Besides, he was a sick man and knew he did not have long to live.)

I'm sure of it, Ernesto said, without compromising himself further. Which grade have you reached?

The seventh, said Ilio with feigned nonchalance.

See, you are good! Do you want to be a concert violinist?

Of course I do, Ilio answered, as if to say: Yes, of

course I'd like a 'fourpenny tart'. — My parents are keen for me to start in an orchestra next year, but I don't want to do that: I'm scared of spoiling my technique.

Don't you go to school?

Not any longer, I left the technical institute after the third year to concentrate on the violin. I used to play a bit before too, but on my own, no lessons . . . My father's an artist, perhaps you've heard of him.

Oh yes, said Ernesto, not needing to lie, for Ilio's father was a respected genre painter who exhibited in a *de luxe* stationery shop (still there today) where he made plenty of sales. Sometimes he was noticed in the newspapers. But life was growing harder for him all the time; apart from himself, he had a wife and three children to keep on the income from his pictures and the drawing lessons he gave in a government school and, privately, to a number of young ladies. (Ilio had three sisters, and the youngest, Luigia, the one he had wanted to beat out of jealousy — or as he put it, *for the honour of the family* — was the apple of her father's eye.) Ilio despised him, partly for using art cynically, to make a living, but more because he would not acknowledge his son's vocation as a great concert violinist of the future, and send him abroad — God alone knows *how* — to study at a famous foreign conservatoire. Though he was contemptuous he did not like other people to criticize him, and was grateful when Ernesto said he knew his father's name, if not his work.

Do you want to be friends? Ernesto asked abruptly.

Ilio was silent for a moment, perhaps taken aback by the question, and he blushed.

Gladly, he said, and again, as at Ondricek's concert, he seemed to be smiling at the angels. This time Ernesto had the smile all to himself.

I'd love to hear you play, he said.

You can if you'd like. I'm learning one of Chopin's *Nocturnes* arranged for solo violin at the moment, by myself. (Ilio was a romantic, the opposite of Ernesto.) Eckhardt (their teacher) doesn't want me to; he only wants me to play scales and exercises, or little bits of Bach at most, but I get bored. This time next week I should know it by heart, then I'll have a word with my mother and invite you home.

In the mean time, said Ernesto, who would not be able to wait so long to see him again, couldn't we go somewhere this coming Sunday? Are you busy?

Sunday? Let me think . . . — Ilio knew he was free as a bird, but he wanted to make Ernesto fret, though he could not have explained why; he liked him, as we said. No, I'm not busy.

So let's arrange for Sunday, Ernesto said quickly, as if worried that Ilio might change his mind. Do you like Barcola or Sant' Andrea better?

This was a crucial question. Since San Bortolo had changed its name to Barcola, it had become the sophisticated spot on the sea front, whereas Sant' Andrea was always a lonely walk, for hardly anyone went there. Ernesto always asked this question when he wanted to put someone to the test, to find out if he wanted to know him better or not. (He had never asked the man because he never wanted to go for walks with him.) If the person preferred Barcola, that was that — and no reprieve. If not, they might then go for the walk. The triangular-faced apprentice, needless to say, would have chosen Barcola. Ernesto was on tenterhooks.

I like Sant' Andrea better, Ilio replied candidly, with no idea how much interest there was in his decision. I don't like Barcola at all, he added, and it's too crowded on Sundays.

With Ilio's answer — with everything — Ernesto

was in seventh heaven. There was a sweet warmth in the other boy's company; he would never be deprived of it again. But the teacher was waiting, and an inner voice warned him not to show too much emotion at what was only their first meeting. They agreed where to meet on Sunday, directly after lunch (never had his guardian uncle's florin seemed so providential: he would be able to offer his new friend a lemonade, or cakes, or whatever he wanted), and he said goodbye with a final reminder not to forget. Ilio willingly promised.

Two boys passing the time on the steps outside their violin teacher's room, talking about their lessons and shaking hands as they part: it would have seemed a banal enough fact of daily life to any passer-by. But thanks to the particular constellation watching over them, and because of its farflung results, this was (everything else apart) a rare encounter: an event such as happens in one country only once every hundred years, if even once.

# Afterword

We can follow Saba's excitement, rapid progress, and subsequent frustration with *Ernesto* in his correspondence with family and friends through the summer of 1953. The first mention comes in a letter to his wife, dated 30 May and sent from a clinic in Rome (in his last years he often retreated to clinics and nursing homes, first in Rome, then in Gorizia, where he died on 25 August 1957).

> I've finished the first episode; really it could stand by itself. Everyone I have read it to — Linuccia, Carlo Levi, Bollea, and a young patient here — says it's the best thing I have ever written (I think so too). But I'm afraid it is unpublishable, because of the language . . . If I could carry on (but I'd need two years of complete peace and quiet — preferably here in the clinic — to finish it), the book would be called *Intimacy*. Some hope! But what I've done so far is so beautiful, people are crazy about it. It's as if a dam inside me had breached, everything flows so spontaneously . . . At most, the story (if I don't manage any more) or novel (if I finish it) might be published in a very small private edition — and then, of course, only after my death.

From another letter the same day:

> (The whole story is imbued with maternity: I even had the distinct impression I was pregnant myself as I was writing it.) And now what? The story could be

developed into a novel: then it would be called *One
Year* instead of *One Month*. It's all in my head now.
But where can I write it? I need peace and silence . . .

To his wife again:

I think 'poor Ernesto' (he is the protagonist — a boy
who was sixteen in Trieste in 1898) will have to
make do with a single month of literary life . . . If
only the story (which is *very pure*, but with a purity
that people don't understand) could be published,
even the first three episodes by themselves (which
they cannot be, for reasons of language), I do believe
that this time I would make some money . . .

To his daughter, 20 July:

Today I must buy myself a typewriter; then I'll write
you a long letter. But will I be able to finish *Ernesto*?
Extremely unlikely: it takes hardly anything to
create an atmosphere which is alien to him.

To Linuccia again, from Trieste now, 25 July:

Ernesto, my Ernesto, wants to emerge whole into
the light. The second part of the fourth episode is
now done, after much sweat and struggling . . .
Will I ever finish the story? It's like a contest between
my weariness and discomfort (I can't bear being in
the shop because of the terrible stench of drains) and
the terrible longing for the book to be finished —
finished and in your hands. Still six months' work at
least, and hard work too. No, I shan't manage it.
Something (weariness apart) is bound to come along
which will keep *Ernesto* unfinished.

And again, 1 August:

But will I finish *Ernesto*? It would need so little to kill
him — I mean, to change the state of mind necessary

for his growth. And that 'so little' could happen so easily . . . I did a bit more yesterday but it's becoming more difficult all the time.

To his friend, the novelist Piero Quarantotti Gambini, 20 August:

I don't know how to describe it; it's like a contest between me and catastrophe, between me and death. I feel that the least irritation, the tiniest bit of grit — and life is shot through with irritations and grit — would make it impossible to carry on. And I'm so tired too; so tired I sometimes think I'm near to collapse. (If you come to Trieste I'll read you an episode: so far, in three months roughly, I've done a hundred pages: I should have finished it in Rome, in the clinic where I began it in a fit of maternity. A poem is an erection; a novel is a birth. But this is difficult to explain by letter.)

To Nora Baldi, 24 August:

How could you ask me if I've reached the death of Ilio yet? Don't you realize it will take a year at least? — always granting I can go on; the work grows more difficult by the day, it's frankly impossible. And that 'little one' keeps tugging at my sleeve, pleading with me not to tell the story of his little goat, etc. Oh God, what am I to do?

Everything will be explained and justified with the death of Ilio and Ernesto's discovery of his vocation. But in the mean time? In the mean time I talk to him by myself just as Ernesto will talk to his shade in the penultimate part of the last episode. He will tell him how good he is, how brave too (in reality he was the victim of a marvellous woman who failed to understand only one thing about him: that he was still too young and delicate to take on a

family) . . . Both of them were married by then, Ilio
no less than Ernesto, to whom a daughter had been
born not long before. And he tells him he has lost
nothing by dying young, describes all the horrors
breeding in the world, says that his sons, now
growing up, would probably have been ungrateful
(as he had been to his own father, whose profession
was not what it is in the novel); that it is nature's
way; that one day, just to hurt him, they might even
have dragged out the story of the little goat . . . [See
Notes to p. 117]

To Piero Quarantotti Gambini, 25 August:

The truth is, I'm sure I can't finish it. The book . . .
is both joyful and ruthless — ruthless in overcoming, in the part I *have* written, every possible
inhibition. (I knew as soon as I'd written the first
sentence that this wouldn't be for publication.)

To Nello Stock, 2 September:

I have finished the fourth episode of *Ernesto* and
started the fifth. The meeting between Ernesto and
Ilio on the steps outside their violin teacher's room is
perhaps the most beautiful moment in the story so
far, although it is *very* hard to explain why.

According to Linuccia Saba, her father continued to
work on his story, rewriting and rearranging some
sections, as well as excising redundant autobiographical details. The last mention of *Ernesto* comes
in a letter to her, 27 August 1955:

I'm never going to have the strength or spirit to
conclude that little unfinished novel I left with him
[Carlo Levi, author of *Christ Stopped at Eboli*, a close
friend of daughter and father] on the strict condition

that he would burn it as soon as I instructed him to do so. Pass on that instruction now, I beg you, without any 'buts', then send me a telegram — DONE . . .

PS I've just this minute rung Carlo. *He doesn't want to but he will*. Don't you for pity's sake throw a spanner in the works.

If the complete edition of his letters currently in preparation is unlikely to shed more light on the reasons for the unfinished state of *Ernesto*, this is because Saba seems to have persuaded himself that it was something it never could have been: a novel. No amount of tinkering or pruning could give his story the impersonality of fiction or the structure of a novel. Whether or not *Ernesto* is factually autobiographical is interesting but beside the point; autobiography breathes in every line: it isn't a question of data. In other words: Ernesto is Saba, yes — but the labourer, Signor Wilder, Tanda, and Signora Celestina are Saba too, for all these characters are wrapped in his embrace. Saba mediates every encounter, qualifying every thought and observation, filling every space in his narrative.

If there is a genre to which *Ernesto* conforms, perhaps it is the genre of *poet's prose* invented by Susan Sontag in her discussion of Marina Tsvetaeva:

> Poet's prose not only has a particular fervour, density, velocity, fibre. It has a distinctive subject: the growth of the poet's vocation. Typically, it takes the form of two kinds of narratives or essay-narratives. One is directly autobiographical in character. The other, also in the shape of a memoir, is the portrait of another person (often of the older generation, and a mentor) or a beloved relative (usually a parent or grandparent). Homage to others is the complement

to accounts of oneself: the poet is saved from vulgar
egoism by the strength and purity of his or her
admirations. In paying homage to the important
models and evoking the decisive encounters, both in
real life and in literature, the writer is enunciating the
standards by which the self is to be judged.

Poet's prose is mostly about being a poet. And to
write such autobiography, as to be a poet, requires a
mythology of the self. The self described is the poet
self, to which the daily self (and others) are often
ruthlessly sacrificed . . . Much of poet's prose —
particularly in the memoiristic form — is devoted to
chronicling the triumphant emergence of the poet
self . . . Poet's prose is typically elegiac, retro-
spective. It is as if the subject evoked belongs, by
definition, to the vanished past . . . In prose the poet
is always mourning a lost Eden; asking memory to
speak, or sob. A poet's prose is the autobiography of
ardour.

But the last word is Ernesto's, in the form of a letter to
Tullio Mogno written after Saba had abandoned his
story. In 1932 Mogno, a mathematician and philo-
sopher who had no personal acquaintance with Saba,
sent him a thirty-page letter about his poetry, showing
'an understanding which in Italy, and at that time, was
miraculous. It was as if Mogno had, purely as a critic,
*lived* my entire poetic existence.' Ernesto's letter is a
strange exercise in juggling identities and time; like a
Borgesian game, except that it is curiously private,
almost self-communing, like the last pages of the story
proper.

*Trieste, 22 September 1899*

Dear Professor Mogno,

Pardon me if I take the liberty of writing to you before I have had the honour of an introduction, but Signor Saba just read me your marvellous essay about the poems you say I shall write when I grow up. Of course, I was amazed and happy to know that I will make such beautiful things and find all those rhymes, which at the moment look way beyond me. But at the same time your essay made me very sad as well — so sad I burst into tears, as if I was still ten years old, not sixteen at all — almost seventeen.

If you want to know why I cried, it's because I realized I'm never going to be head clerk in a colonial trading company, or a great violinist either; no, it's my fate to be a poet. You wouldn't believe how miserable this made me, especially about the violin. When Signor Saba finished reading out your essay I made up my mind to abandon the violin for ever; I felt so sad as I kissed it goodbye, I thought how like the dying Faust I was. Farewell, sweet dreams of glory . . . What's more, I discovered — again thanks to your essay — that only a few people will like my poems, and then only much later, when I'm as old as uncle Giovanni (he's my guardian as well).

Unfortunately I can't understanding everything you say about me and the poetry I'll write one day, even though Signor Saba did his best to explain it all. Of the poets who — if I follow you correctly — will be my masters, I've only read one so far, Leopardi — and to be quite truthful only one poem, 'Saturday in the Village', which was in our Italian reader at school (now I am — was, rather — apprenticed to a business, and it doesn't even have anything to do with colonial trade). I had to learn it off by heart and recite it in class, which I did very well I think — I only faltered twice. But the others all laughed at me and my way of saying the lines. Not the master though: he doesn't much like me, but he not only approved of my reading, he even punished a boy who was laughing too grossly — the idiot tried to get even by passing it on that he'd be waiting for me outside, afterwards. Vincenzo Monti's *Aristodemo* and Alessandro Manzoni's *Adelchi* were in the same book and I read them too, partly because I felt I ought, partly for pleasure. I don't know anything by Alfieri yet — or only a few lines, which uncle Giovanni recites after dinner. You can guess what uncle Giovanni is like! He's not exactly nasty (he gives me a florin every week) but he *is* mad — should be locked up! Because I have to tell you, Professor Mogno, that I'm a socialist, and uncle Giovanni can't stand socialists. He's married, luckily, and only comes here for Sunday dinner. Our arguments always start after we've eaten, and sometimes he even threatens to clout me round the head (he only dared do it once; the argument was about socialism, of course, and my mother fainted from shock, so uncle Giovanni never tried a . . . 'repeat performance'). He accused me of having no fatherland; which is not true, because I love Italy very much, and it's one of the greatest dreams of my life to die in a war against Austria so that Trieste can be an Italian city. But my uncle was with Garibaldi when he was young and he can't tolerate any talk about socialism now. What about you, Professor Mogno, what do you think about socialism? I would be very glad to have your opinion on this matter. I had better admit, I tried to read *Capital* by Carlo Marx a few months ago, but was very bored; probably I'm still too young to understand such a profound work. I read a socialist newspaper instead — *The Worker* — which I like a lot. *The Worker* says Garibaldi would be a socialist if he was alive today. I don't really know what to think, and there's no one to help me: I've only got Signor Saba, who's very old, and anyway he doesn't like talking about politics, at least not with me.

But getting back to poetry, I should also tell you that I have written several poems already, though I've never thought I would ever become a poet. The last time was a year ago; I still remember it all (it was very long — more than two pages), but I'd be afraid of boring you if I were to copy it out here. This is how it starts:

> Oh cameretta, cameretta mia,
> che mi fosti compagna del dolor

> [Oh little bedroom, little bedroom mine,/that kept me company in all my suffering.]

and it ends with these two strophes:

> Ma ricomparve il tramonto sol,
> e rinnovò le cose con l'amore.
> La farfalletta ha dispiegato il vol,
> con insperato, ma potente ardore.
> E d'ogni cosa me facea un trastullo,
> nell' April della vita tutto d'or.

> [But then the set sun reappeared,/and all things were renewed by love./The little butterfly unfurled its flight/with potent and unhoped-for zest./And everything's my toy, my sport,/in this, life's golden-burnished April.]

I have never read this poem to anyone except my cousin, whom my mother detests. At first he said I couldn't have written it; then he admitted that maybe I could (I had to swear to make him believe me), but it would only have been any good if the rhymes had been difficult. He says a poem is as good as its rhymes are difficult. I don't know if you agree with him; I'd like to know your opinion of that as well — it would certainly be more valuable than my cousin's, as he is still at school and only three months older than me.

I just said before that I am employed — apprenticed to a business in Trieste. Was, rather: it ended two days ago. My employer and I weren't on very good terms anyway, and then he signed another apprentice without telling me, when there wasn't any need — and made him sit at my desk! You wouldn't believe how awful the new boy was! So I used the excuse that my employer was begrudging me money for the tram when I had to go to the port and back several times a day; I wrote him a rude letter which I put on his desk, and then he had no choice but to give me the sack (which was what I wanted). But I could see he was almost reluctant to do it: he made a scene and flapped the letter under my nose, calling me a 'crazy, mannerless boy' and nearly crying at the same time. Maybe he was waiting for me to beg his pardon. When I told Signor Saba the whole story he was hugely amused and put it straight into the book he's writing about me. This book tells everything about me, even the things that shouldn't be told; but he's sworn never to publish it, he'll only read it to two or three trusted friends when it's finished. Let's hope 1) he never finishes it, and 2) if he finishes it, he keeps his word.

Now I'm free of the boring routine of going to the office every day. By a stroke of luck I've made — *hope* I've made — a friend. He's a little bit younger than me (fifteen and a half) and still wears short trousers and has long hair. I saw him a few nights ago at a concert by Ondricek, the violinist, and I knew straightaway he was a violinist himself, but far better than me, he really *is* destined to be a great artist. I wanted to say something that evening at the Music Society, but I couldn't find him anywhere on the way out. But — see if there isn't such a thing as fate! — we met face to face the next morning on the steps outside my violin teacher's rooms, and it turned out we have the same teacher. We started talking right there, and now we're going to meet this coming Sunday. Just think, Professor Mogno, he would rather go to Sant' Andrea, where hardly anyone goes these days, than to Barcola, which is swarming — just like me! I'm very fond of him already, I know, and I hope he's fond of me too. As soon as I woke up this morning I told my mother (she always brings me coffee and milk in bed, since I was badly ill with tummy aches) I had found a friend. She said that I'd have done better to find a job; you can imagine how terrible *that* made me feel. My mother does love me, but she doesn't understand me; which is another reason I so liked the part of your essay where you talk about the adolescent nobody loves, who seeks refuge in the secret world of his dreams. That's a perfect description of me. And I was feeling so good when I woke up — really happy! Last night, just before dawn, I dreamed I could fly. I was flying around my little room (the one in the poem) so high I nearly touched the ceiling, and it was so marvellously easy I couldn't think why everyone wasn't flying with me; I told Ilio (that's my friend) that he should try it. And he did, soon he rose from his bed — in my dream it was in my room with me — and there we were, flying to-gether, both of us. I described all this to my mother; she only shrugged, but I was happy all the same — so happy I scrambled out of bed just as I was, with nothing on but a shirt, and turned three somersaults on the bed for joy. My mother was indignant: she said I was making a spectacle of myself — it was indecent at my age, and she would fetch the carpetbeater (!) if I did not get back into bed that instant. 'Oh mother!' I said, 'you never laid a finger on me when I was little, and you're threatening me now when I'm almost seventeen.' Signor Saba came to find me later; I told him my beautiful dream too, and he jotted it down so he could put it in his book later. He said that flying in dreams has a precise meaning (but didn't want to tell me what it is); but I don't believe dreams are trying to tell you anything. What do you think, Professor Mogno? Do you believe in dreams?

Please excuse all this chatter; I'm sure all I've done is use up your valuable time. (Even my mother tells me I chatter too much.) Signor Saba is the only person who says I never talk enough when we're together. But I don't know if he means it or if he's pulling my leg.

Thank you again for your essay; I take it as a good omen, and I forgive you for depriving me of my illusions of becoming a great violinist. (To tell the truth I had worked it out for myself.) I hope my new friend Ilio becomes one instead. (As long as he doesn't forget our date, we'll be going for the walk only the day after tomorrow — I'm already ticking off the hours.) His triumphs will more than make up for my own 'fiasco'.

Yours sincerely,
Ernesto

PS I don't like to lie to Signor Saba, or tell him less than the whole truth, but it might be better not to tell him that I have written — at least not yet. But if you do tell him, please let me know. Also I would be very glad if you reply to this letter.

PPS My friend's real name is Emilio, but his family all call him Ilio and we agreed I should call him that too.

The reason I'm a little bit worried about him keeping our date is this: he already has a girlfriend of his own, even though he's so young and still wears shorts (Signor Saba says his parents make him wear shorts to save money). They go out together, but nobody else knows. He showed me a photograph of her in secret, and promised to introduce us. And he promised he would invite me to his house to hear him play one of Chopin's *Nocturnes* arranged for violin, as soon as he knows it by heart. He's learning it by himself (our teacher doesn't even know). He must be so good, when you think he's reached the seventh grade already after starting so late (he was thirteen). Not like me! Signor Saba tells me I don't quite have the right idea about Ilio (he wonders if he isn't a bit of a rogue); but he doesn't forbid me to see him — he knows it wouldn't work. Anyway he believes young people have to live their own lives. Excuse me again for going on so long.

And those poems you say I'm going to write one day, I'll have to write them myself, Signor Mogno, not you.

# Thanks and acknowledgements

To John Berger and Chatto & Windus Ltd for permission to quote from G., Chatto & Windus 1972; to Denys Mack Smith and the Michigan University Press for *Italy, A Modern History*, Michigan University Press 1969; to Nicholas Powell and David Higham Associates for *Travellers to Trieste*, Faber & Faber Ltd 1977; to A. J. P. Taylor and Penguin Books for *The Hapsburg Monarchy 1809–1918*, Penguin Books Ltd; to Susan Sontag and the Virago Press for the Introduction to *A Captive Spirit: Selected Prose* by Marina Tsvetaeva, Virago 1983.

For help of all sorts, to Daniele Archibugi, Petra Brauns, Anna Fano, Luca Fontana, Marioleena Freeth, the Museo Provinciale di Gorizia, Richard Huckstep, Claudio Magris, Rosanna Marino, Robyn Marsack, Stelio Mattioni, Serena Maude, Michael Schmidt, Noel and Christine Thompson, Ian Thomson, Alessandro Vaciago, Daria Viviani and her assistant at the Comune di Trieste, and Giorgio Voghera.

# Notes

p. 9   *Now that I am old. . .*

The epigraph is a self-quotation, the first sentence of Saba's own memoir of a visit to Gabriele d'Annunzio in 1907, which he published in *Ricordi-Racconti* (Memories-Stories, 1956), a book of prose pieces.

The young Umberto Poli was an admirer of d'Annunzio. His first choice of *nom de plume* was highly d'Annunzian — 'da Montereale', which was dropped almost immediately in favour of 'Saba', adapted from Sabaz, the name of his beloved nanny. (*Saba* also means *bread* in Hebrew: a coincidence which he, who, after his flirtation with d'Annunzio, wanted his poetry to be as simple and essential as bread, must have approved.)

p. 9   *in dialect, like the ones which follow*

Dialect looks as well as sounds very different from standard Italian, so Italian readers know at once which of the two is being spoken, which matters for two reasons. First, because the story is so sensitive to ways in which articulacy is an index of class and social power; then, relatedly, because Saba presents the dialect as the language of emotional vitality and openness. The labourer cannot speak Italian, and is embarrassed by Ernesto when he misunderstands the words 'Ali Baba'. Tanda the prostitute speaks dialect. The mother unknowingly lapses into dialect in Episode Four, when she 'sends morality to the devil' and gives her son the manifest love he needs. Ernesto himself is competent in both dialect and Italian.

Luckily for the translator, these crucial moments are made explicit in the narrative, so do not need to be rendered by the language alone. I have tried to bring into English the colloquial rhythm, succinctness and delicacy which mark Saba's use of dialect; for he does not use it naturalistically. He thought his story would remain unpublishable because of the occasional coarse expressions, but any reader now will be struck more by the tact of the conversations between the boy and the labourer than by any crude *verismo*.

Even if I were able to put *triestino* into an 'equivalent' British dialect, I doubt that I would have done so: in so far as they still survive, British dialects do not stand in the same relation to standard English as Italian dialects to Italian. Tuscan Italian was adopted as standard by the new republic a century ago, and, while the dialects have been increasingly diluted and marginalized, they are still mutually incomprehensible. People from different parts of the country still communicate in the standard Italian they learned in the classroom and hear on television and radio, not the dialect they talked in the playground and probably at home.

Trieste has produced a number of dialect poets, most notably Virgilio Giotti, much admired by Pasolini, and Carolus Cergoly; but no one claims that their idiom is the authentic *triestino* of the streets. (According to Voghera, Giotti spoke beautiful Tuscan, never dialect, and Saba 'hardly ever' spoke dialect.) In all the great length of the *Canzoniere* there are only a few phrases of dialect, and not many more in his collected prose – indeed, it is too limited and limiting a medium for anything more developed in prose than short sketches or anecdotes.

p. 9 *(just the colour of some poodles' eyes)*
A private joke; Saba's daughter Linuccia had a poodle called Baruch. Saba wrote to his wife that Ernesto (who, remember, was 'a dog, not a cat') behaves 'something like Baruch, something like an angel.'

p. 11 *Her least of all . . .*
Ernesto's bizarre family situation corresponds almost exactly to that of Saba himself, whose parents' marriage was arranged by a marriage broker. His mother, Felicita Rachele Coen, was Jewish; his father, Ugo Edoardo Poli, Catholic. 'The day I was born (a Friday, March the ninth 1883),' Saba wrote to a friend in 1955, 'my father was in prison for *lèse majesté* (Franz Josef): but I think it was to get away from my mother, especially as the money had run out and the relatives did not want to give them any more. When they came to put a blanket over me, my mother kept them off, saying *If he lives, he lives, and if he dies, he dies . . .* (My mother was not ignoble, but she did not know how to live, nor how to let other people live.)'

As a boy Saba lived with his mother and his aunt Regina, with his 'terrible uncle' a regular visitor to the household. His relationship with his mother, to whom he addressed many early poems, was passionately close. As an adult he came to see that he had misjudged his father, his first meeting with whom is remembered in this sonnet from the sequence *Autobiografia*:

My father, *assassino*, so I thought,
until I met him in my twentieth year,
and knew him for the child he was, and saw
that for the gift I have I have him clear.

My own blue stare upon his face I caught;
a smile, for all his troubles, ear to ear.
Forever the world's pilgrim; what he sought,
by more than one girl nourished and found dear.

He was a gay one and light-hearted; my mother
felt every weight and burden of her life.
He slipped away from her like a balloon.

She used to warn me, 'Don't be like your father.'
I understood it in me later on:
they were two races at an ancient strife.

p. 12 *They soon go, either in cake shops . . .*
Giorgio Voghera remembers Saba's own partiality for Ernesto's favourite food: 'When he wanted to buy cakes or pastries Saba usually went to one of the best, most expensive *pasticcerie*; no butter was pure enough for him, and he invariably suspected the baker of substituting *margarine* (a word he could not pronounce without horror).'

p. 14 *and I'm always for the socialists*
The period between about 1890, and the advent of Fascism in the early 1920s, was one of vigorous activity and expansion for the left in Italy. The *Partito socialista italiano* was founded in 1892, and in the universities and in print, Marxist ideas were disseminated by a new generation of philosophers. In modern Trieste the debate was characteristically intense — some of its flavour can be found in James Joyce's letters to his brother.

The reader can get an idea of what socialism meant then to a boy of Saba's/Ernesto's age and temperament from Benedetto Croce's remarks in his *History of Italy from 1871 to 1915*: 'socialism conquered all, or almost all, the flower of the younger generation . . . To remain uninfluenced by it, or to assume, as some did, an attitude of unreasoning hostility to it, was a sure sign of inferiority.'

p. 16   *she always says you can't get ahead without German*
Under the Austrian administration the official language in Trieste was Italian, but business at the higher levels was often conducted in German, for a simple reason: 'The majority of the funds of Triestine shipping companies, insurance corporations and credit associations was in the hands of purely Austrian or Austro-Slav concerns, so that Italian money played a relatively unimportant part in the development and activities of the ports.' (Moodie)
    Slovenes had no choice but to learn German or Italian, preferably both, if they wanted to benefit from the Triestine boom.

p. 18   *with a passion for Germany* . . .
The overwhelming public issue between 1870 and 1914, for non-Slavic and even Slavic Triestines, was irredentism: the 'redemption' of what were dubbed the 'unredeemed lands' of Trieste and the Trentino by appropriating them for the new republic of Italy.
    'The chief trouble which spoils Trieste is politics,' wrote Lady Isobel, wife of Sir Richard Burton, British Consul from 1872 to 1890. 'When we went there an Austrian would hardly give his hand to an Italian in a dance. An Italian would not sit in the concert where an Austrian sang. If an Austrian gave a ball the Italians threw a bomb into it: and the Imperial family were always received with a chorus of bombs — bombs on the railway, bombs in the gardens, bombs in the sausages: in fact it was not at such times pleasant.'
    Another contemporary British witness: 'In Trieste . . . almost every nationality is represented; but while the Italians form the majority [i.e. a majority of people chose to tell the Austrian census officials that Italian was their first language], there is, among the middle and especially the commercial classes, a considerable proportion of Germanic Austrians. The feud between the two is as incessant as that between the Germans and the Czechs.' (Palmer)
    Not that all Italians were irredentists: the business community knew very well that it thrived courtesy of Austrian trade and investment. It was the intelligentsia, including the

artists, and the professional class, which were by and large irredentist.

p. 19   *with serene innocence*
*con tranquilla innocenza* — the very phrase used in the epigraph.

p. 26   *You* are *like an angel to me*
Saba's affection for boys was well known to his circle of friends, and is often apparent in the *Canzoniere*, but it seems unlikely that he had affairs with them. Clearly the question arises whether as a boy or young man Saba ever had a relationship with an older man. Giorgio Voghera refers discreetly to 'certain tendencies' which the poet had 'as an adolescent, and which returned in his old age', and so far as I am aware, nothing more definite is known, or available in print at least.

The most important of these passionate friendships bears closely on *Ernesto*. While staying with his friend and colleague Emanuele Almansi, a Jewish Piedmontese antiquarian bookseller, before the war, Saba met his son Federico (1924–79), and, then or later, fell in love with him. From a letter to his daughter Linuccia, in 1948: 'it occurs to me very often that he is not materially a young man at all, but an angel in human form come to earth to give one final comfort to my last and in all other ways despairing years.'

Saba's love appears to have been consciously Socratic; he encouraged the boy to write poetry, and contributed a preface to his first and only collection (*Poesie*, Florence 1948). He also addressed him as Telemachus in a famous poem of his own; and he is clearly the subject of the poem 'Angelo' (Angel), and the young man of 'Vecchio e giovane' (Old and Young).

These three poems date from 1945–48. In 1949 Federico showed the first symptoms of a serious mental illness. Around the same time his father suffered financial ruin; he tried to kill his son, then himself. He failed, and Federico, whose condition was anyway deteriorating irreversibly, was committed to an asylum.

Federico's madness came as a 'mortal blow' to Saba, and was largely responsible for the chronic unhappiness of his last years. Is not *Ernesto* an attempted reparation in art for damage that could not be undone in life? The man in the story does no harm to the boy — on the contrary, his love serves, however unintentionally, to bring him nearer to self-consciousness; that is, to his vocation as poet.

p. 31   *Tu* and *lei* are the second and third person singular personal pronouns, used in respectively the informal and formal modes of address — the equivalents of *tu* and *vous* in French.

p. 32   *books from the Biblioteca Economica Sonzogno series*
This was a series of cheap, pocket-sized primers of economics, political science, etc.

The excursions into bibliography in *Ernesto* are inexplicable without the knowledge that Saba was for more than thirty years the proprietor and manager of a bookshop (new and antiquarian) in Trieste, and to him these details were not at all esoteric. (He bought the business, which guaranteed him some sort of income for life, in 1919, out of his Aunt Regina's legacy.)

The books he mentions — usually at crucial moments — are the texts in Ernesto's sentimental education: pointers by which Saba charts Ernesto's unconscious movement towards his vocation.

p. 35   *There was a bird cage. . .*
The perceptions of animals and their separate animal existence are a constant pleasure of Saba's poetry and prose. 'Like the child,' he wrote in his *Storia e cronistoria*, 'the poet loves animals, which, by the simplicity and nakedness of their lives, far more than men who are constrained by social necessity and continual pretences, are "close to God", that is, to the truths that can be read in the open book of creation.'

Saba's love poetry often involves birds. His famous poem — it is almost, as he himself admitted, a hymn — to his wife, Carolina Woelfler, written soon after their marriage, compares her successively to a hen, a cow, a bitch, a rabbit, a swallow, and finally to an ant. This is the opening comparison:

· *To my Wife*
You're like a creamy pullet,
my white hen,
whose plumes the wind disturbs
when she stoops to drink
or peck at the ground,
yet proceeding over the grass with measured step
just like a queen:
full-bosomed and superb

and better than roosters;
she is like all the females
of the peaceful animals,
close to God.
And so if eye and judgment
do not fool me,
among these your equal will be found,
and in no other woman.
And when the evening makes them comfortable,
the peaceful cluck of their troubles
reminds me of you
complaining
and unaware
that like the hens
your voice makes sad and gentle music.

One of his last collections, dating from 1948, is called simply *Uccelli* (Birds): brief, limpid poems with such titles as 'Robin', 'Doves in the Piazza delle Poste', 'Blackbird', and — the last poem he wrote to his wife — 'This Year . . .', about the autumnal departure of the swallows. (The moment later in the story when Ernesto flings himself on his bed, oblivious to Pimpo's song, might have been taken from a lyric in *Uccelli*.)

p. 36 *when he started reading* The Worker *despite his uncle's prohibition . . .*

*Il lavoratore* (The Worker) was the official organ of the 'Adriatic Section of the Socialist Party in Austria'. After the Italian Socialist Party split in 1921, *The Worker* allied itself with the new *Partito communista italiano*; the novelist Ignazio Silone (*Fontamara, Bread and Wine*) worked for the paper for a while. Trieste was a city of political extremes, with a proud radical tradition on the one hand, and on the other, immediate, comprehensive support for Fascism: 'The first demonstration of importance by an actual Fascist unit of which I find newspaper record was the burning of the Nardoni Dom, the headquarters of the Slav nationalist organisation in Trieste, on July 13, 1920.' (Beals)

The young Saba certainly professed himself a socialist, and before the First World War published poems in *The Worker*. His friend Amedeo Tedeschi was an editor there, and Scipio Slataper, the author of *Il mio Carso* (1911), a wonderful, headlong poem-in-prose about growing up in and around Trieste, contributed too.

p. 40 *he would imagine Ulysses . . .*
The paired names of Trieste and Ulysses automatically imply a third: that of James Joyce. Yet Homer's voyager was equally important to Saba, who in several poems about his childhood compares himself to Ulysses, and in a late lyric speaks through him:

### Ulysses
In youth I sailed along the Dalmatian coast.
Great islands bloomed on the wave; above them flew
once in a while a bird in search of prey;
covered with kelp, and slippery, under the sun
they shone as beautiful as emeralds.
When, in the night and the high tide, they vanished,
with our sails underwind we ducked for the deep
to flee that perilous snare. Today, like that,
my kingdom is No Man's land. My harbor
burns lanterns for foreigners; and I turn back to sea,
pressed ever on by my unbeaten spirit,
and by this brokenhearted love of life.

(As one would expect, Saba's Ulysses has more in common with Tennyson's 'grey spirit yearning in desire' than with Joyce's Bloom — 'not to say that he had ever travelled extensively to any great extent but he was at heart a born adventurer though by a trick of fate he had consistently remained a landlubber except you call going to Holyhead which was his longest.')

Incidentally Saba's friend, the novelist Piero Quarantotti Gambini, said that the *Canzoniere* is more than 'a book of songs': it is 'a sort of *Odyssey* of man in our times.'

p. 44 *he never reads the* Piccolo . . .
*Il Piccolo della sera* — a newspaper founded in 1881 by Teodoro Mayer, one of the likely models for Bloom, whose background was as typically Triestine as his name: he was the son of an Hungarian Jewish postcard-peddler who had settled in the city.

Signor Wilder would not have read the *Piccolo* because of its political sympathies, which were so emphatically irredentist that its offices were a routine target for the more violent *austriacanti* whenever there were disturbances.

By 1914 it had achieved a daily circulation of one hundred thousand, and it remains Trieste's leading paper. It was edited

by Roberto Prezioso, a friend of Joyce, who contributed
occasionally; and then by Silvio Benco (1874–1949), Saba's first
influential advocate — he wrote a preface to his first book in
1911 — and an excellent literary journalist. Like *The Worker*,
the *Piccolo* was a nursery for many Triestine writers.

p. 45 *Certainly I do and I love her . . .*
Saba's nurse was Peppa Sabaz, a Slovene woman who had lost
her own son in infancy. Saba spent much of the first four years
of his life in her home, while his mother worked at menial jobs
in the city. He took his name from hers and addressed several
poems to her. Her house on Via del Monte became an emblem
of security and unconditional love: a *paradiso* he had known and
lost irrecoverably.

p. 46 *He had just come by way of the Boschetto*
Formerly a wooded hill at the edge of the city, the Boschetto
(literally, 'little wood') was enclosed by urban expansion in the
late nineteenth century and finally destroyed after the last war.
Saba himself, and some of his bedside audience, would have
known that it was a favourite place with courting couples.

p. 51 *that very substantial category of people who cannot imagine a
brilliant career not being prefaced by a university degree.*
On 21 June 1953, just a month after completing the First
Episode of *Ernesto*, Saba attended a ceremony at the University
of Rome to receive a *laurea honoris causa*. His speech of thanks is
touchingly wholehearted; Saba never felt accepted — never *was*
accepted — by the *borghesia* (as Italo Svevo, for example, the
successful manufacturer/novelist with his motor car and fur-
collared overcoat, was); his lack of a university education was
no doubt a significant shortcoming in class-ridden Trieste. The
speech shows how possessed he was by memories of his youth,
and by his mood of reconciliation, while writing the story:
'. . . I should like to end with a short account of a complex
memory of my schooldays, a memory which is, for me, linked
inseparably to this honorary degree. When I was fourteen years
old I was a pupil in the fourth grade in the Dante Alighieri
School in Trieste. My classics master, who was also our form-
master, generally passed for — and in part actually was — one
of the 'harsh but fair' brigade. Now as everybody knows, boys
love these harsh-but-fairs; they did in my day at any rate, and I
loved this man. A word of praise and I melted — all the more as

his praise was so infrequent. It so happened that he took a sudden loathing to me, for reasons he never made clear. Perhaps loathing is too strong — the right word would be *antipathy* . . . I did not and at that age I could not take any interest in Greek and Latin as such; I only studied to please my mother and my form-master: in other words, to bring me the love of the people I needed. (Another poets' flaw: depending too much on other people's love and approval, and reacting strangely, even violently, when they are deprived of that love and approval.) So, as soon as I realized that I was not only no longer approved but was actually unpopular, I fell almost overnight from a place near the top of the class to one somewhere near the bottom. This was at the very end of the school year of 1896–97, and my final mark in Greek would decide whether or not I advanced to the next grade. Still, however anxious I was and grief-stricken, I pored over my textbooks hour after hour; for family and other reasons I couldn't permit myself the luxury of being what we scathingly called "a repeater". My fate would be settled by the last composition of the year, to be written in class under the master's watchful eye — watching to stop his pupils copying from each other. I finished the composition and was almost sure I had no mistakes, or hardly any. But a doubt (all too justified, alas!) lingered deep in my heart, and nervously, too nervously, I waited for the day the master would give back our exercise books with the mistakes underlined in red and the verdict at the bottom of the page. When Franz Josef was Emperor, school marks were scaled not by number but in words, and this is how they ran (I'll remember them as long as I live): *Excellent, Very Good, Good, Satisfactory, Poor,* and *Unacceptable.* I no longer aspired to *excellence*: that was beyond my reach, I knew inside myself and also by the expression on my form-master's face. But I felt sure — *almost* sure — of being *good.* The day of which we were so frightened that finally we longed for it to dawn, dawned. The teacher handed every book back to its pupil owner; no one was so audacious as to read the mark straightaway: we each covered the page with a sheet of blotting paper, which we drew more or less slowly down . . . our hearts sinking lower at every glimpse of red. Good grief! How seriously we took everything in those days and at that school! I had the satisfaction of seeing red only once — it was nothing bad, little more than a spelling mistake really, in the first sentence. I was expecting a *Very Good*, a *Good* at worst.

And a *Good* would have guaranteed my promotion . . . I spare you any account of my emotion when I reached the bottom of the page only to discover an *Unacceptable* in that terrible red ink — for a single, paltry, irrelevant mistake! The worst mark of all — even the most idiotic of idiots weren't declared *unacceptable*. My despair enhanced the joy — tactlessly obvious, I thought — of the boy beside me. His name was Diem, and he, with more mistakes than I, had been granted a magnificent *Very Good*. (He is one of the few survivors of my generation, and I salute him now and wish him many more years of life — if he wishes for them himself.) I wanted to put my hand up and request an explanation, and perhaps I should have done so, but when Franz Josef was on the throne, who dared speak to his superior unless he had been spoken to? — And what a superior at that! He settled everything soon afterwards in a talk with my mother: he would secure my promotion by lavishing a *Very Good* as my final mark in Greek, provided the poor woman promised to take me away and enrol me in a different establishment. And indeed, as he gave me my final report, this harsh-but-fair looked me straight in the eye and said in front of the whole class, "We can only hope you will be more successful at your new school." Awful words, which were to have an almost crucial effect on my tormented existence.

'I made a lovely bonfire of my classics books, which lack of love had made so difficult, in fact quite impossible.

'For a short while I attended the Imperial Royal Academy of Commerce and Nautical Science, then took a job in the hope of becoming (it was my dream at the time) a good, upright and respected businessman.

'All this is one of the reasons I am so grateful to you, illustrious scholars and dear friends. The degree you confer on me today cancels that *Unacceptable*, that, I swear, undeserved *Unacceptable* from my memory and from the face of the earth. And at the same time I feel that I really have forgiven my classics master, who has been dead such a long time now. It's true I have forgiven him many times before, like Renzo with Don Rodrigo [in *I Promessi Sposi*, the novel by Alessandro Manzoni]. "But", asks Fra Cristoforo, to make Renzo understand that his previous pardons were not heartfelt, therefore neither complete nor, from his point of view, meritorious, "but how many times have you forgiven him already?" No, this time I forgive him once and for all.'

A few days later Saba wrote to his friend Bruno Pincherle: 'Oh God, if only I could have read them *Ernesto* instead of that little speech . . . I think everyone there would have gone mad with joy, even the venerable Chancellor, who must be pushing eighty hard. People, *Bruno mio*, need, they so urgently need to "make themselves at home" — to be freed from their inhibitions. What else should be my task in old age?'

p. 51   (*years later* . . . *he would call it not sweet but* passionate)
Saba is quoting one of his own best-known poems, 'Il borgo' (The Town), published in 1926, in which he recalls an epiphanic moment of more than twenty years before; in a mood of deep depression, the twenty-year-old Saba was watching workers file out of the factories in one of Trieste's new suburbs (the town of the title), and was suddenly possessed by a longing to break out of his own self, to make himself part of the *communità umana*:

> . . . In lui la prima
> volta soffersi il desiderio dolce
> e vano
> d'immettere la mia dentro la calda
> vita di tutti,
> d'essere come tutti
> gli uomini di tutti
> i giorni.

[There for the first/time I knew the sweet/vain/desire to immerse my life in the passionate/life of all,/to be like all men of all/days.]

Saba returns again to this seminal moment when Ernesto sees the workers at the factory gates: '*All comrades, all socialists,* thought Ernesto, wanting to be one of them.'

p. 53   *Learning the violin . . .*
The young Saba aspired to learn the violin, and came no nearer to succeeding than Ernesto. He recalled this adolescent ambition in a poem published in the volume *Ultime cose* (Last Things, 1944):

*Violin*

Got
for some colored stamps in a trade

and quiet
for so long, what sweet and silver sounds
I scoop from your wood tonight,
my violin:
           I raise
in a difficult time the mirage
born of you; I loll in the troubled dark;
and though you were not a gift,
        in dreams I get born again
through you, from time to time, of an evening.

p. 58   *ruled solely by the sensuality of the moment*
After his own analysis in 1929–30, which he saw as the turning
point of his adult life, Saba was a wholesale, doctrinaire convert
to Freudian theory. His analyst was a former pupil of Freud,
Edoardo Weiss, the first Freudian analyst to practise in Italy.

A shelf of books has been written on the place and impact of
psychoanalysis in Triestine culture; interested readers of Italian
should look for *Letteratura e psicoanalisi* by Michel David
(Milan, 1967).

Is not Ernesto a sort of incarnation of Freud's 'polymorphous
perversity' — protean, spontaneous, guiltless infant sexuality?

p. 58   *without a licence from the police*
In his autobiography *The World of Yesterday* (London, 1953),
the Austrian novelist Stefan Zweig describes the semi-legality
of prostitution in the capital of the Austrian empire at the turn
of the century: 'A girl who had decided to become a prostitute
was given a particular concession by the police and received her
own book as a qualifying certificate. Inasmuch as she submitted
to police control and complied with her duty of being
examined by a physician twice each week, she had acquired the
business right to lease out her body at any price she saw fit.'

p. 60   *on his way home from the Dante Alighieri School*
Saba attended the Ginnasio-liceo Communale 'Dante Alighieri'
from 1893 to 1899.

The Triestine novelist Giani Stuparich (1891–1961) was a
pupil and later a teacher at the school. 'The "Dante Alighieri",'
he wrote, was 'the nursery of the intellectual and ruling classes
of Trieste. From this school emerged nearly every one of its
illustrious citizens – doctors, teachers, lawyers, engineers too,
who held high the name of Trieste throughout Italy and be-

yond. The story of the "Dante Alighieri", which celebrated its fiftieth birthday in 1913 with a community of more than 800 pupils, is the story of Trieste itself.'

But it is very unlikely that Saba ever contemplated his alma mater in such glowing terms.

p. 61    *But Ernesto was different . . .*
As with the passage in Episode One about the boy's future 'style', this is a case of Saba praising his own poetry in the way which, he believed, critics should have done yet so rarely did. Bitterly resenting this critical neglect, incapable of ingratiating himself with the literary establishment (whose headquarters were anyway so far from Trieste), Saba came to believe, or to console himself with the belief, that he, like Nietzsche, would be born posthumously. More practically, he also gave a lead to the critics by writing his *Storia e cronistoria del Canzoniere* (History and Chronicle of the *Canzoniere*), a 337-page commentary on his entire poetic output to date, written in the third person, published under a transparent pseudonym in 1948: perhaps the most extraordinary case of a poet creating or at least broadcasting the terms in which he wants to be understood.

p. 62    *So she was a Slovene from the Territory*
'The Territory' was the administrative *Land* — called the *Küstenland* or Littoral — comprising Trieste, Gorizia, Gradisca and Istria.

'Wedged between the Italians and the Germans,' as A. J. P. Taylor puts it, the Slovenes were the largest Slavic group in the Austrian empire. The majority of the population in the *Küstenland*, including Trieste, was of Slovene stock, though often Italian-speaking. There was a great influx of Slovenes into the city during its boom; Slovene labour built the railways, manned the ports, and filled the lower ranks of the civil service.

Taylor concludes that 'With the passage of time and the blurring of distinction between historic and non-historic peoples, Trieste would, no doubt, have become Slovene, as Prague had become Czech and Budapest Magyar; the Slovene misfortune was to have arrived at consciousness too late in the day. The Italians, aware that their majority was fictitious and precarious, used the arguments of wealth and superior culture which the Germans used in Bohemia; the superior culture was shown in a similar violence and intolerance.'

p. 62 *Ernesto's pleasure . . . even before he was born.*
In 1945 Alberto Moravia published a short novel, *Agostino*, about a boy's initiation into the knowledge of sex. This is how Agostino hears the facts of life from a sophisticated older boy: 'Speaking slowly and using gestures to make himself clear that were precise without being at all coarse, he explained to Agostino what he now felt he had always known and had somehow forgotten, as in a deep sleep.'

But the new knowledge affects the boy catastrophically: 'He was obscurely aware that this disastrous day had brought him into an age of difficulty and unhappiness, but he could not imagine when he would get free of it.' And: 'it seemed to him that he had bartered his old innocence not for the assured, manly condition he had been dreaming of, but for a confused, hybrid state in which, without any kind of compensation, new repulsions were added to the old ones. What was the use of seeing yourself clearly if this clarity only brought new, more impenetrable darkness?'

Agostino tries, like Ernesto, to solve his problems by going to a prostitute, but his attempt is a fiasco. The story ends with the boy in blank despair, certain that his misery and guilt can never be allayed.

Saba read the book as soon as it appeared and wrote this note for his book *Scorciatoie e raccontini* (Short Cuts and Little Stories, 1946):
'THE CASE OF MORAVIA: I have just been reading *Agostino*. It is a good book: the author's best so far. It encompasses, explains, and is stronger overall than his previous work. But it is a *bad* book too, a book which would have been better not written. IT DOES DIRT ON LOVE.

'Unfortunately all Moravia's work is like this. One might say that his characters take no delight in the thing which — as Euripides has it — yields mortal men their most precious pleasures. Moravia's lovers (they are actually haters) go through, or rather force themselves to go through the motions of love, as if they can *only* be motions of resentment and mutual disgust. I repeat: they DO DIRT on love — they DEFORM it.

'Moravia's readers see that he is up to all sorts of wilful mischief; the public at large calls him "licentious"; the critics argue among themselves; the moralists either preserve a contemptuous silence or stiffly condemn. The "case" of Moravia is altogether simpler than this, and so obvious as to *crever les yeux* [put your eyes out]. Something *must* have happened to him (and not only to him . . .); not today, not yesterday, but in prehistorical times, buried in complete (but not therefore eternal) oblivion. It is as if, when still a baby, he had secretly watched (while pretending to be asleep, perhaps) what the author of THE HYGIENE OF LOVE (another madman, but this one had no talent) droolingly calls "sexual congress"; which he mistook, as wide-eyed infants can, for an act of aggression or even sadism. This made a very powerful impression on him. Later he forgot, but was without knowing it already *fixated* on that monstrous, dream-like image. I do not know if it has marked his life (nor do I wish to know), but it marked his art — this much I *can* say.

'And it is a pity, for Moravia is not merely talented — it's possible he is a writer of genius: this is the impression left by *Agostino*, anyway. What's more, he is a well-intentioned person (sometimes — God forgive his innocence — even a moralist). Can no one tear the deadly image from his retina in the nick of time? transform a child's curse into an adult's blessing? in a word, *cure* him?'

(The other 'madman', incidentally, is the prodigious Paolo Mantagazza (1831–1910), founder of the first general pathology laboratory in Europe, anthropologist, novelist, parliamentarian, and author of such advanced tracts as *The Physiology of Love* (1873), *The Physiology of Pleasure* (1880), and in 1876, *A Day in Madeira, or The Hygiene of Love*.)

*Ernesto* is Saba's answer to *Agostino*: a denial that first experience of sex can be truthfully interpreted in terms of purity/ impurity, innocence/corruption. Agostino has been in some sense mutilated by the advent of sex in his life, whereas Ernesto's relationship with the man, and his heterosexual initiation with Tanda, are not only liberating stages in his growth, the growth of a poet's body-and-soul, but also a boon to the two adults.

In *Ernesto* no hurt is irremediable. How a reader reacts to this enchanted innocence, the essence of Saba's story, will depend of course on everything that reader is. Here are two eloquent critical opinions; first, Elsa Morante:

'This is a story about a boy's first experiences of sex — rather, of sexual love. They start, quite by chance, with one of those relationships which our superstitions make taboo, for all that they are real, human, and natural. But Saba's ideal boy,

borne along by his innocent sensuality, his spontaneous
curiosity about life, is immune from certain taboos which turn
natural reality into grotesque, destructive monsters . . . Saba
does not shun any detail, however difficult or secret it may be,
if he thinks it is necessary to his story: he does not *purify* so
much as a word. Yet things which other people cannot say
without making them obscene or sordid, he reveals in their true
clarity as natural and innocuous . . . Any explanations of this
phenomenon must come back to this: Saba has something
without which there can never be realism or liberty in art (as in
history itself), but only slavery and rhetoric — he has fun-
damental respect for life and for human beings.'

Now the Triestine critic Claudio Magris, for whom this
'immunity' is bought at too high a price, and this beauty is not
truth:

'*Ernesto* is certainly proof of great courage and *joie de vivre*.
But Saba knew that innocence, especially *his* innocence, can no
longer be serene and spontaneous. Saba's innocence is jealous
and aggressive, difficult and turbid, cruel and precarious: it is
the innocence of someone who accepts life whole in all its
sweetness and ferocity, like the birds in his late lyric poems
which sing but also seize their food with fury . . . We no longer
live in an earthly paradise, and no one knew this better than
Saba. In his poetry the anxiety and evil of life are kept at bay
but hardly; whereas in *Ernesto* he is attempting a global ab-
solution of life, affirming that everything is inevitable and all
remorse is wrongheaded . . . The anarchic, savage foundations
of life, which, in one of his superb late poems, Saba sees in the
truth of the animal that knows no shame or sorrow, rather
tends in Ernesto to melt away in idyll, and begins to look like a
most improbable goodness.'

The other story to which *Ernesto* is, so to speak, an obvious
antidote, is *Death in Venice*; but there is, to my knowledge, no
evidence that Mann's symbolistic fable of inversion and death
was present at any level of Saba's mind when writing his tale of
life and liberation in Trieste.

p. 62  *He felt like a man arriving home after a perilous voyage . . .*
Ulysses again, safely restored to Ithaca, his childhood home.

p. 63  *When he rose from the bed, heartened*
Even the post–coital variety of tristesse is banished from the
world of *Ernesto*.

In 1946, soon after the new *Canzoniere* was finally published
by Einaudi, Saba had resorted again to the figure of Ulysses in a
poem about his brief exultation:

*Mediterranea*
I think of that sea far off, a harbor, hidden
ways of that city where once I was
who am here now, raising my hands to the gods
in supplication:
may they wish me no punishment
for one last triumph I now despise
(though my heart, for the sweetness of it, almost quits);

I think of a tawny siren
— kisses delirium joy — ; I think of Ulysses
who rises in that land from his sad bed.


p. 64    *The city was spreading in all directions . . .*
Like an ageing Bourbon monarch, the body of Trieste has
shrunk within its imperial finery, and all the efforts of Italian
governments since the 1920s to find a role for it commensurate
with the grandeur of its architecture and the resources of its
people cannot change its fortunes; Trieste was developed to
serve Austrian imperial trade, and without it, has no function.
Grass pushes between the flagstones of the piazza where
Ernesto went to hire the day-labourer; the only boats at the
quays of the old port now make circular trips around the
harbour; and a huge banner is draped over the august façade of
the Palazzo Lloyd: LLOYD ADRIATICO IN LOTTA PER LA
SOPRAVVIVENZA DI TRIESTE MARITTIMA — 'fighting for the
survival' of Trieste as a port.

In the 1890s, when Saba and Ernesto were growing up, the
city was thriving. 'There are', Nicholas Powell rightly claims,
'few cities where the urgent sense of drive of the nineteenth
century, that age of commercialism, can more easily be re-
captured than in Trieste.' When Austria lost its north Italian
provinces in 1859, Trieste became the empire's principal
Mediterranean port. The Südbahn railway from Vienna had
been open for two years; the completion of the Suez Canal ten
years later improved Trieste's mercantile prospects even
further. There was massive Austrian investment; the New
Port, finished in 1883, was built and equipped almost entirely at

Austrian expense, and large subsidies were paid to the main shipping companies.

'It may be concluded that in every economic respect modern Trieste is an Austrian creation, although its population is mainly Italian and Slovene. Its hinterland was primarily Austrian, its railway communications were constructed at Austrian expense, and the great majority of its shipping flew the Austrian flag.' (Moodie)

The population expanded from 66,000 in 1848 to 220,547 in the census of 1910. Also in 1910, A. L. Frothingham published his *Roman Cities in Northern Italy and Dalmatia*, and these help-less sentences show the sort of impression Trieste made in its heyday: 'Ancient Tergeste is now the modern busy sea-port of Trieste, main outlet of the Austrian empire on the Adriatic, seat of the Austrian Lloyd Steamship Company. It is so absolutely modern that it seems almost hopeless to attempt to trace any of its Roman life.'

The young Saba was proud of his new city; witness his reaction when he visited Florence in 1905: 'it's a dead city, corrupted by outsiders and the lack of industry and business.'

p. 67    *and probably in piazzas the small world over*
*tutto il mondo-paese*: Saba is making play with a proverb, *Tutto il mondo è paese*, meaning: All the world's a village.

p. 69    *today he would be called a patriot but not a nationalist*
'There was no general doctrine of irredentism, but *ad hoc* argu-ments were devised to serve each immediate political purpose . . . The irredentism which looked toward Trent, Trieste, even sometimes to Nice, Corsica, and Malta, was in one sense a projection of *risorgimento* patriotism. But where Cavour spoke of the country's good, Crispi [Prime Minister 1887–91 and 1893–96] spoke rather of its greatness and its predominant position in the Mediterranean. In 1894 Farini, the president of the Senate, talked of the army alone keeping Italy united, and he had ominously remarked that Italy must become a strong militarist state or cease to exist.' (Mack Smith)

Saba is here taking care to distance Ernesto from the oppor-tunist excesses of irredentism, which condoned anti-Slav racism, and later discredited itself for ever by clamouring for Italian intervention in the Great War; and from the excesses of Italian nationalism after the Second World War, demanding an Italian Trieste at any cost.

p. 69   *he harboured no loathing for the Slavs*
'It was the last city — or the first, depending on which way you
were travelling or fleeing — where the virtues of European
protocol, honour and production could almost be taken for
granted. On this point both the Austrians and Italians of Trieste
were agreed.' (Berger)

If they could agree on little else, they knew that Trieste
should not belong to the Slavic majority. It was a case, to use A.
J. P. Taylor's sarcastic terms, of 'historic' peoples assuming
their superiority over 'non-historic' peoples. The Italians no
doubt viewed the Slovenes as potential rivals for future owner-
ship of Trieste; the Austrians were eventually prepared to use
the Slovenes as a stick to beat the ever more unruly Italians: 'In
1913, Trieste was ordered by Prince Hohenlohe to dismiss
Italian-speaking employees not of Austrian nationality. Formerly, the Italians had looked toward Vienna for protection
against the advancing Slovenes, but a novel Austrian solicitude
for the Slavs now threatened Italian livelihood as well as Italian
culture and language there.' (Mack Smith)

Roberto Bazlen remembers: 'Faced with these people, the
Italians felt their superiority to the full — a superiority based on
a school certificate, on their lives all insured with the Assicura-
zioni Generali (that was a world in which everyone insured
everything), and on their trading contact with foreign lands,
and they did nothing to hide it . . . Swollen with this
superiority of theirs, they tended to despise them (the word
*Slav* was an insult) simply for the fact that they did not understand Italian until they learned it (but how dumbfounded they
would have been, had the Slovenes despised them for not
knowing Slovene), and this moved them to silent, brooding
resentment.'

This tripartite racism is powerfully evoked by John Berger in
the scene when G., an Italian, provokes a scandal by taking a
Slovene girl to the Austro-Hungarian Red Cross ball:

'An Italian has brought a Slovene to the ball. A Slav girl from
the villages, dressed outrageously in pearls and muslin and
Indian silk. When she dances the waltz, she dances like a
drunken bear, clutching her partner close to her and thumping
with her feet.

'A young officer in a blue uniform gravely informed a white-
haired gentleman that he was willing to challenge the interloper
who had had the temerity to insult His Imperial Majesty's Red

Cross. The white-haired Viennese was a general who had fought at Solferino. If he spoke German, my boy, you would be justified. But they tell me he has nothing but Italian. And in that case I must forbid you.'

Saba loathed racism. In 1948 he published an article, 'If I was Governor of Trieste', in the *Corriere della sera*, in which he declared that he would introduce only one piece of new legislation: the death penalty for anyone and everyone who incites racial hatred.

p. 72 *he would die in a gas oven* . . .
Saba's shock at the first news of the death camps is registered in a note dating from February 1945: 'AFTER NAPOLEON everybody was a little bit *more*, simply because Napoleon had existed. After Maidaneck . . .'

(Is this the earliest instance of that numb wordlessness which Adorno later insisted — 'No poetry after Auschwitz' — is the writer's most authentic, appropriate response to the holocaust?)

p. 73 *What a beautiful city Trieste is, thought Ernesto for the first time in his life.*
Trieste is as intrinsic to Saba's work as Dublin to Joyce or Paris to Baudelaire, and this, in effect, is a valedictory salute.

His letters display every sort of judgment, opinion and feeling about his city, from blessing to condemnation; it is the most dismal city in Italy, a blasted, deathly place, and it is his *citta adorata*! But beyond approval and disapproval, it is simply his city, of which he could write truly, near the end of the Second World War, in the poem '1944':

I had a lovely city, set between
the jagged mountains and the gleaming sea:
my own, that I was born there, and still more
my own that I discovered her as a boy,
then as a man forever made my own —
I married her to Italy in song.

It needs to be remembered that Trieste's fate was not settled until nine years after the end of the War. It was contested by Yugoslavia — Tito's partisan army had liberated the city — and the USSR on one side, and Italy and the Allies on the other. There were violent demonstrations and rioting in the streets by the different factions as late as 1954, when, thanks largely to the

estrangement between Tito's government and the Soviet Polit-
buro (which was distracted by internecine power struggles
after Stalin's death), a memorandum of understanding was
finally signed in London in October, securing the city and a
connecting strip of coast for Italy. Only then did Allied troops
withdraw.

Saba was convinced and terrified that Yugoslavia would win
Trieste. He had always tended to identify his city with himself,
and in *Ernesto* — written in 1953 — the poet's tenderness
toward his own youth, or simply toward 'youth', is not dis-
tinguishable from tenderness toward Trieste in its lost prime.

p. 74    *and Diem — the boy he used to sit next to at school*
In his speech at the University of Rome (see above) Saba
mentions this schoolmate: 'His name was Diem'. . . More
proof of autobiography — as if any were needed — or might it
be evidence of Saba's possession *by* the story he was writing at
the time?

p. 75    *I'm no 'baba' . . .*
A pun which could only be attempted in English by resorting
to the American slang 'babe', *baba* being Triestine dialect for
'girl'.

p. 75    *reading* The Arabian Nights *as he lay . . .*
'Any one of importance who passed through Trieste came of
necessity to the Consul of world-wide fame. Indeed, it is no
exaggeration to say that the Consul at Trieste was more of a
personage in his way than the Ambassador at Vienna.'

During his Consulship, from 1872 to his death in 1890, Sir
Richard Burton, 'the greatest Orientalist of his age', made his
translation of *The Arabian Nights*, published in 16 volumes by
the Kamashastra Society of Benares, 1885–88.

With his polyglottism (he spoke 21 languages), his margin-
ality, restlessness, and scandalous fascination with erotic texts,
Burton surely felt an elective attraction to Trieste, where he
lived longer than in any other place. (Quotations from Dodge)

p. 77    *facing the Teatro Communale (now the Teatro Verdi)*
Now, as Saba says, simply the Teatro Verdi, the Teatro Communale became the Teatro Communale 'Giuseppe Verdi' by
unanimous vote of the city council on 29 January 1901, the very
day of the composer's death; and the first monument to Verdi
anywhere in Italy was erected in Trieste.

These acts were a final homage to an artist whom Trieste had adored for half a century. Two early works, *Il Corsaro* and *Stiffelio*, were written for Triestine theatres; his wife was born there; and most importantly, he was irredentism personified. His name was even an irredentist acronym — *V*ittorio *E*manuele *Re d'Italia* — and whenever his work was performed in the last quarter of the century, the evening was liable to be disrupted by explosive chants of *Viva Trieste italiana! Viva Verdi!*, which the *austriacanti* would try to drown with shouts and chants of their own, until the imperial authorities restored order.

John Berger cites or invents a typical incident: 'According to gossip, Marika, Wolfgang von Hartmann's wife, had had not long ago an Italian lover who was forced to leave the city. He was a musical conductor and he provoked a public scandal by arranging a concert at which the first syllable of the title of each work, as printed in the programme, spelt out an anti-Austrian slogan. Most of the audience were Italians and they soon spotted the message, gave the conductor an ovation, and at the end started shouting VERDI! VERDI! . . . As a result, the conductor lost his post at the Conservatoire and left the city.'

p. 80   *He didn't like the trams now they were no longer horse-drawn.*
The first rails for horse-drawn trams were laid in 1876 by Cimadori & Vilturelli of Belgium. 'The city could well be proud, for this tramline was opened only a year after the Paris tram service, and only eight years after the very first tramline network in Liverpool,' writes a local historian, whose desolated peroration shows that he more than shares Ernesto's regret: 'On 24 September 1900, an electrified copper wire banished horses from the tram rails of our city. A new century had arisen to devastate the serenity of a vanished age. Never again would the bucolic, silky rustle of the traces spread sweetly through the air, respecting even the post-prandial slumber of the coachman-charioteer on his seat, gathered into the arms of Morpheus as he rode by the sunny pavements and colonnades of old Trieste.' (Rutteri)

p. 80   *A carriage would have been better . . .*
'Especially in summer, Saba liked to make the journey from his bookshop in the via San Nicolò, to his home some ten minutes' walk away, by carriage. I can see him now, borne blissfully along the streets of Trieste at a gentle trot, reclining alone

across the seat of the open carriage, a half-smoked Tuscan cigar in his mouth, a smiling, daydreamy expression on his face.' (Voghera)

p. 82    *that climate which breeds revolutions*
'The climate is detestable, varying from arid heat in summer to a succession of continual gales in winter.' (Dodge)
    These 'continual gales' are the *bora*, a north-easterly winter wind which beseiges the city in three-day blasts, bringing clear skies, bright light and foul tempers.
    Roberto Bazlen said that, for all the unrest in Austrian Trieste, 'the *bora* was responsible for violence far worse than any perpetrated in civil disturbances — one of the few cases in history when the elements were more destructive than man!'

p. 91    *the only sphere of public life . . . which openly and stubbornly refused to function*
We are so accustomed to images of the Austro-Hungarian empire as a system in entropy, sinking under its own weight towards the nemesis of 1914, that one suspects Saba of irony; but no. Although his sympathies, like those of almost all Triestine artists, were with the irredentists, Saba was not alone in feeling — at least with hindsight — that life under Austrian rule was also, at a mundane material level, agreeable. Roberto Bazlen again: 'Austria was a rich country, with an all-inclusive, pompous officialdom which could, to be sure, seem pedantic and absurd . . . but still, it functioned perfectly, manned by its steady, slow, conscientious civil servants, incorruptible on the whole and with a religious awe for the laws of the state — partly because they were well paid and had no need for tips, charity or blackmail to reach the end of the month; on the state salary one could live not at all badly by the standards of the time — and more than well by those of today. An old friend of mine in Trieste, for example, the first person of real culture I ever knew, was employed at the Post Office — he wanted to be left in peace, had no career ambitions, and by spending his working life right up to retirement behind a counter, he could afford to live in a four-room flat, collect a beautiful library of several thousand volumes, most of them leather-bound; purchase a violin and a grand piano; marry, and provide his son with a good education; go to the café or have a glass of wine every night; go to the theatre; take a month's holiday abroad every year — and all this on his salary. Now it might seem odd that a

truly cultivated person could adjust to life as a humble state
employee, and at the very time when doors were opening to
everyone, but in Austria such a thing was not only possible, it
was an ideal solution for people who did not want to fight for a
living, who had other things to occupy their minds; a life of
slow, tranquil work and little responsibility which ensured all
the necessities of life, and not only the material ones — it was
not a sterile existence . . . I never heard people talk about
unemployment until after the Great War; before, anyone who
did not have enough initiative to set to work on his own
account (and it needed little enough at that) could find himself a
job the same day he began to look, and would be embarrassed
by the choice . . . Taken all in all Austria was fair and tolerant,
because it was old and had a ballast of age-old experience, and
commanded all the dignity of its moribund ceremonial.
Equality before the law of all the subject peoples of the empire
was recognised in the constitution; and the bureaucracy, ever
faithful to the constitution, did not, if truth be told, abuse its
power.'

p. 96    *at the edge of the old city*
The *Cittavecchia*, the 'old city', on the site of Roman Tergeste.
Still unmistakably the heart of Trieste, in 1898 it was quite
separate from the new port and burgeoning suburbs. Saba
celebrated the *Cittavecchia* in this poem from the book *Trieste e
una donna* (Trieste and a Woman, 1912):

### Oldtown
Often, to get back to my house, I take
an obscure road in the old part of town.
The puddles fling the yellow lamp-light up,
and in the street there is always a crowd.

Here, in the midst of all that's going on,
from inn to shop or brothel, and the crush
of men and merchandise in a great port,
I find again, as I go passing through,
the Infinite that is humility.
Here is a prostitute with her sailor, the old man
who stands there cursing, and a stammering crone,
a soldier seated at the fishfry stand,
a jilted girl who cries out terribly
for love, for love —

they are life's creatures, sorrow's, everyone;
there beats in them, as in myself, the Lord.

Here, with the humble ones for company,
I feel my spirit mend,
stand pure in the humiliated street.

p. 105   *streetcorners in Rena Vecchia*
Rena Vecchia was the busiest, scruffiest, most clamorous
quarter of the old city.

p. 105   *when he read* Cuore *by Edmondo De Amicis . . .*
The best-known Italian children's book, *Cuore* (Heart) was
made a prescribed text in the new republic's state schools soon
after its publication in 1886, and is still widely used as a reader.
Countless thousands of Italians have been brought up on this
collection of stories about a school year, which were intended
by De Amicis (1846–1908) to strengthen the moral and
patriotic fibre of the nine to thirteen age group.

Reputedly the book is still read in Central and Eastern
European schools. In his *Record of a Life*, Georg Lukács'
reaction to *Cuore* marks the beginning of a healthy in-
dependence of mind: 'My scepticism was directed at the legend
that poor boys were good scholars and outstanding people.
This myth was purveyed on every page of De Amicis' book,
which was much read by children at the time.'

(UNESCO has sponsored a new translation of the book:
*Cuore, The Heart of a Boy*, London, 1986.)

p. 109   *an incorrigible optimist/activist*
My efforts to identify this mysterious person met with no
success. My own hunch is that he means the great novelist Elsa
Morante (1918–85). A close friend in the last decade of his life,
she was certainly one of the few people to whom he read the
story aloud; and she — a Communist Party member until 1956
— was equally certainly an 'activist', taking part in protest
actions against the *latifundia* (vast estates owned by absentee
landlords in the south of Italy) and in the 1960s making
polemical speeches for the anti-nuclear movement.

p. 110   *not at the Schiller Club (where the German colony met) but at
the Music Society, which was an Italian, indeed an irredentist
circle*

Founded in 1823, with its own theatre from 1845, the *Società filarmonico-drammatica* became the social and cultural focus of the *borghesia patriottica*.

After sunset on 28 August 1914, the day Austria-Hungary declared war on Serbia, the state employees, bankers and merchants of the German-speaking community crowded into the Piazza Grande, where the Schiller Club flew the flags of the Triple Alliance from its windows and a military band played the Imperial Anthem.

p. 112   *a certain learned man* . . .
Saba is sniping at one Attilio Hortis (1850—1926), a scholar and irredentist. The first Italian Triestine to be elected — in 1897 — to the Vienna Parliament, he wrote forgotten studies of Boccaccio, Petrarch and the humanists.

Honoured as one of the worthies of Trieste in the proudest years of its history, and representative of both unimpeachable patriotic virtue and stolid intellectual effort, Hortis is exactly the sort of establishment figure with whom Saba was never at ease; by whom he always felt, and was, undervalued; of whose popularity he was helplessly envious.

p. 116   *the delectable hill of Scorcola*
*la dilettosa erta di Scorcola*: the adjective is Dantesque, from the first canto of the *Inferno*. Virgil identifies himself to Dante, then asks

> *Ma tu, perchè ritorni a tanta noia?*
> *perchè non sali il dilettoso monte*
> *ch' è principio e cagion di tutta gioia?*

But you, why do you come back to such disturbance?
Why do you not climb the delightful mountain
Which is the beginning and reason of all joy?

(trans C. H. Sisson)

p. 117   *Ilio was the boy* . . .
Ilio is Ugo Chiesa, who played the violin and was a year or two younger than his devoted friend Saba.

Ugo introduced him to his girlfriend, Lucia Pitteri, with whom Saba proceeded to fall in love. They agreed to write when Saba went to Pisa in 1903. Ugo discovered Saba's letters; Lucia broke down and had to be hospitalized; Ugo told Saba their friendship was over, and swore revenge. Saba was tormented by the fear that Ugo would denounce him to the authorities and doom him to prison and exile, on the basis of a couplet in a poem which rhymed *Absburgo* with *spurgo* (phlegm!) — 'at the time it seemed to me an incredible *trouvaille'*. He knew the fear was absurd, but this did not stop him becoming obsessed. He always believed that his adult neurosis — which psychoanalysis illuminated but did not cure — stemmed ultimately from this first irrational terror.

In the event the two young men were reconciled, without ever regaining their old intimacy. Ugo and Lucia married; they both died young, in 1913 and 1919 respectively.

One may guess that all the complexities of plot and, more importantly, of Saba's still-unresolved feeling, partly explain why he abandoned his story so soon after the advent of Ilio and the woman with corn gold hair, who would, we know from Saba's letters, have been the Lucia figure (see the Afterword).

p. 120   *Do you like Barcola or Sant' Andrea better?*
The fishing village of San Bortolo was developed into a seafront resort in response to the needs of the swelling urban population. The Passeggio di Sant' Andrea is a long avenue on the southern edge of Trieste, above the New Docks.

p. 121   *thanks to the particular constellation watching over them*
Which might be the stars in this constellation?

At seventeen (Ernesto's age now) Saba had written a self-consciously Leopardian poem, *Alla mia stella* (To my Star). So large and beautiful, so alone in the heavens, the star reminds the boy of his first love, and at the same time comforts him by its very separateness from his and everyone's troubles, and seems to know the secret of his future.

Reviewing Stuparich's first collection of stories, Eugenio Montale began: 'So the influence of Trieste's lucky star in the new literature of our country still persists . . .'

What, then, is this constellation watching over the two boys, but love, poetry, and the spirit of Trieste itself?

# Bibliography

| | |
|---|---|
| Ara, A. and Magris, C. | *Trieste, un' identità di frontiera* (Turin, 1982) |
| Bazlen, Roberto | *Scritti* (Milan, 1984) |
| Beals, Carleton | *Rome or Death, the Story of Fascism* (London, 1923) |
| Berger, John | *G.* (London, 1972) |
| Cary, Joseph | *Three Modern Italian Poets — Saba, Ungaretti, Montale* (New York, 1969) |
| Dodge, W. Phelps | *The Real Sir Richard Burton* (London, 1907) |
| Favretti, Elvira | *La prosa di Umberto Saba* (Rome, 1982) |
| Mack Smith, Denys | *Italy, a Modern History* (Michigan, 1969) |
| Magris, Claudio | *Dietro le parole* (Milan, 1978) |
| Moodie, A. E. | *The Italo-Yugoslav Boundary: A Study in Political Geography* (Liverpool, 1945) |
| Morante, Elsa | 'Sull' erotismo in letteratura' in *Nuovi Argomenti* (1961) |
| Palmer, F. H. E. | *Austro-Hungarian Life in Town and Country* (London, 1903) |
| Pinguentini, Gianni | *Nuovo Dizionario del dialetto triestino* (Modena, 1984) |
| Powell, Nicholas | *Travellers to Trieste. The History of a City* (London, 1977) |
| Rutteri, Silvio | *Trieste: spunti dal suo passato* (Trieste, 1968) |
| Saba, Umberto | *Per conoscere Saba* ed M. Lavagetto (Milan, 1981) |
| | *Poesie e prose scelte* ed G. Giudici (Milan, 1976) |
| | *La Spada d'amore* ed A. Marcovecchio (Milan, 1983) |
| | *Storia e cronistoria del Canzoniere* (Milan, 1977) |

*Thirty-one Poems*, translated by Felix Stefanile (New York and Manchester 1980)

| | |
|---|---|
| Stuparich, Giani | *Trieste nei miei ricordi* (Rome, 1984) |
| Tamaro, Attilio | *Storia di Trieste*, vol 2 (Rome, 1924) |
| Taylor, A. J. P. | *The Hapsburg Monarchy 1809–1918* (London, 1948) |
| Voghera, Giorgio | *Gli anni della psicanalisi* (Pordenone, 1980) |

(The dates given are those of first or most recent publication.)